TAKE ME IN THE DARK

TAKE ME #2

R.L. KENDERSON

NOTE TO READERS

This book is an erotic romance for entertainment purposes only. This story is pure fantasy. Please always practice safe sex and use protection.

PROLOGUE
ADDISON

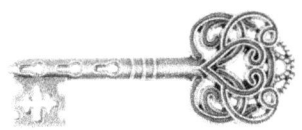

*R*ing. Addison Graham Wolfe shut her bedroom door and answered her phone. "Hey, Olivia," she said as she lay on her bed.

It was Maddox's night to put the boys to bed, so she was going to enjoy a moment of talking on the phone with her friend in peace.

"Hey, Addison. I saw that you'd called. Everything okay?"

Addison laughed. "Yes, everything is fine."

Ever since Olivia Mayer had represented Addison's now husband—then boyfriend—against an attempted murder charge a few years ago, she always asked if everything was okay.

"If I needed your help, I would text you 911 or leave you a *call me back right now* voice mail."

One good thing that had come out of the situation was that Addison and Olivia were closer. In college and law school, they hadn't done much hanging out together outside the classroom besides getting together to study. But since Maddox's arrest, the two of them had become better friends. Addison and Maddox had gone to Des Moines a few times to see Olivia since then.

Olivia chuckled.

"Things are good. Maddox has really settled into his role as the sheriff, and work is the same for me."

"Until you defend someone that your husband has arrested."

"He doesn't do the arresting. His deputies do."

"You know what I mean."

Addison shrugged even though Olivia couldn't see her. "Eh, they're minor crimes. If I had a serious case, I know who to call."

"Is that why you called me?" Olivia's voice brightened.

Addison frowned. "Sorry, no. Aren't things exciting enough for you in Des Moines?"

Olivia sighed. "No…things are good. I'm finishing up a big case, and I cannot wait for it to be over."

That didn't sound like Olivia. She loved going head-to-head in cases.

"Is everything okay?"

She didn't answer right away. "Yes. Everything is fine. Or it will be."

"Are you sure?" Addison was starting to worry.

"Yes, I'm sure. I don't know what's wrong with me."

"When's the last time you took a vacation?"

"Uh…"

"I'll answer that for you. So long that you can't even remember. Why don't you and Ray go somewhere fun? Your firm is big enough now, so you can take a few days off. They don't need you to be there every day to run everything."

Olivia cleared her throat. "Ray and I broke up."

Addison sat up. "Oh no. What happened?"

"It's not important." Olivia's voice said otherwise.

"Are you sure about that?"

Olivia sighed. "It's embarrassing."

"The only person I'm judging is Ray."

"He sent me a text about a week ago to say it was over because I was boring in bed."

Addison winced. *Ouch.* "He broke up with you in a text? Asshole."

Olivia chuckled. "Thanks for not focusing on the *boring in bed* part."

"That's on Ray, not you."

"It's still humiliating, especially when I know what a great sex life you have."

As if on cue, Maddox pushed the bedroom door open and silently walked in their bedroom. Addison lay back down and admired her husband as he stripped off his shirt, showing off his muscular body.

Olivia was right. She did have a great sex life.

If only Olivia could find herself a man like Addison's husband.

Maddox pulled his phone out of his pocket and tossed it on their bed before he shucked off his pants and threw them on the wicker chair in the corner. Addison watched Maddox walk into the connected bathroom and was disappointed when her eye candy was out of sight.

"Addison, are you still there?"

"Yeah, I'm here. You need to find a man who fucks you like Maddox fucks me."

Olivia gagged. "*My ears.* I can't unhear that."

Addison laughed. "I'm sorry. Did I offend your delicate senses?"

Olivia laughed, too. "Yes."

Addison turned onto her side. "I'm serious though." She gasped as an idea came to her. "I know. You need to go on vacation somewhere with a friend, find a single guy that you're never going to meet again, have him fuck you silly, and come home. Maybe if you find someone you'll never see again, you'll let go a little."

Addison felt bad for Olivia and her breakup, but she knew that Olivia was kind of stiff in bed. She had admitted so to Addison. In all fairness, Ray probably wasn't entirely to blame about things ending because Olivia would often put work before intimacy with her partner. Addison understood how important sex was to a relationship. He was still an asshole for breaking up with Olivia through a text message though.

"Are you offering to go on vacation with me?"

Addison closed her eyes and pictured a beautiful beach on the ocean, where the weather was the perfect temperature, and she sighed. But reality set in, and she opened her eyes. "I wish. Maybe when I'm done nursing Thane, we can go somewhere together." Thane was only five months old, and she wanted to make it until he was a year before she stopped nursing. She'd done the same for Spencer, who was now two years old. "I'll just have to make sure not to get pregnant again right away."

"They do make this thing now called birth control."

"You're so funny. I was on the minipill. I just forgot to start back on the regular pill once I stopped breastfeeding. I won't make that mistake again. I have an IUD now."

Addison loved her kids, but if she had another right away, she might go insane.

"Great. Then, let's make tentative plans to go somewhere together. It's summer now anyway. We should do it when it's cold outside and we're freezing our asses off."

"Hmm…Thane will be a year old in February," Addison said with a smile. But she soon lost it. "But that doesn't take care of you now."

"Yeah, but February's not that far away. Right?"

Maddox's phone vibrated on the bed, and a notification popped up.

> Flash: Tickets booked. Will forward flight info. Can't believe I'll be there in just under a month.

Addison grinned as a plan began to take shape in her mind.

Flash was the nickname for Tommy Morelli, a former SEALs teammate of Maddox's. He and Olivia had met once, and while the two of them hadn't exactly hit it off, Addison had sensed some sparks. Plus, if anyone could sex up Olivia, it would be a Navy SEAL. Especially one like Flash, who had gotten his nickname for a reason.

"I have a better idea."

"What is it?" Olivia asked just as Maddox exited the bathroom.

"Why don't you come here for Brook Days next month? Will your current case be over by then?"

Maddox's eyebrows flew up.

"We're on track to be finished with closing arguments in the next two weeks or so. What weekend is Brook Days?" Olivia asked.

Addison told her and added, "But come for more than just the weekend. Come for a week or two. It's not the ocean, but it'll get you away from the city. And we could always go to the lake and sit on the beach if we have the time."

"Let me check my calendar," Olivia said.

"I'll wait."

"Who are you talking to?" Maddox asked.

Addison pulled the mouthpiece away and sat up. "Olivia."

Maddox chuckled and shook his head. "You know that's when Tommy's going to be here."

Addison forced a confused look on her face. "Oh, it is? I completely forgot."

"What did you say, Addison?" Olivia asked.

Addison moved her phone back to her mouth. "Oh, nothing. Maddox was talking to me."

"Oh. So, if my current case is finished and I can get one of the other partners to take a small case, I should be able to make it work."

"That's the best news."

"Are you sure I won't be in the way?"

"Nope. You can stay in my old apartment above my office. No one is renting it right now, so you can have your own space."

And no one was renting the Carson brothers' apartment either. The Carson brothers owned the building next to hers. Being neighbors had worked for her and Maddox. It might influence Olivia and Tommy, too.

"I like that idea."

"*Yes*. This will be so much fun."

Olivia laughed. "Whatever you say. I'd better go. Tell Maddox hi for me."

"Olivia says hi," Addison relayed the message and held out the phone.

"Hi, Olivia," Maddox said loud enough for Olivia to hear.

"See you next month," Olivia shouted.

"Okay, but I just have to warn you—"

Addison quickly brought the phone back to her ear. "Sorry, Olivia, gotta go."

"Wait. What was Maddox going to warn me about?"

Addison fake laughed. "Just the boys. They're a handful. Please say you'll still come."

"I'll still come."

Addison looked over at her husband, who had his hands on his hips. She smiled at him. "Okay. We'll talk later. See you soon."

"See you soon. Bye."

Addison ended the call before Maddox could say anything else and flopped onto her back, her heart racing.

"Addison, what did you do?"

"Nothing. I invited Olivia here for a break."

The bed dipped as Maddox put a knee on it. "Did you purposely invite her for when Tommy will be here?"

Addison winced. "I plead the fifth."

"That's lawyer talk for guilty." Maddox lay down next to her.

"So what if I did? Those two need to hook up."

"Isn't that for them to decide?"

Addison rolled her eyes. "I'm not going to tie them up and force them to have sex. But if they happen to be around each other and get a little turned on…who am I to stop them?"

Maddox shook his head and laughed. "This is going to be a disaster."

"No, it won't. You'll see."

"Okay, but don't get mad at me when I tell you I'm right."

"I won't because you won't say that."

"Whatever you say." Maddox rolled on top of her. "Now, speaking of being tied up and sex…"

Addison threw her arms around his neck. "What do you have in mind?"

1

TOMMY

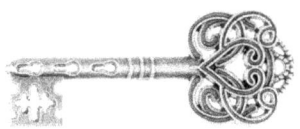

I exited the airplane and pulled out my phone, turning off Airplane Mode. The first notification that popped up was a text message from my friend Maddox.

> Mad Dog: Sorry, running late. The baby wouldn't go to sleep, and I didn't want to leave Addison alone with both kids crying.

I shuddered. Two kids under three. Mad Dog was crazy. It wasn't any wonder he'd jumped at the chance to have me visit.

Don't get me wrong. He loved his wife and his two boys, but I also knew him well enough to know that he was probably climbing the walls.

I could relate. Since my forced retirement from the Navy around four months ago, I didn't know what to do with myself. I had picked up a few odd jobs here and there, but they were boring and nothing like being a SEAL.

So, when Mad Dog had invited me to Iowa, I'd booked

my plane tickets for as soon as the orthopedic surgeon said I would be cleared for a vacation.

My phone buzzed as another text came in.

Mad Dog: I'll probably be an hour late.

Eh. It was just an hour. That was what I got for getting into town late at night. I'd sat longer in the same position, waiting for a signal to take action. Sitting in an airport bar, drinking a nice beer, was like a holiday compared to being overseas and hiding from the enemy.

Me: Text me when you're close. I'll meet you at the curb for Arrivals.

I turned off my screen and slung my carry-on over my shoulder. I didn't wait for Maddox to reply. I knew he had my back.

I headed for the nearest place that sold alcohol. Unfortunately, the Des Moines airport wasn't very big, even with its international status, and I didn't have a lot of options. The food court was out, so I headed upstairs, where I found a bar.

I took a seat, ordered a draft beer, and pulled out a book.

I was two chapters in and half a drink down when I felt someone approach me.

"Whatcha reading?"

One would think that a person holding a book would be a good signal to leave them alone. More often than not, it wasn't.

I marked my page with my thumb and glanced up.

A woman stood before me in an outfit that looked way too uncomfortable for traveling. She wore a short dress with a plunging neckline that wasn't exactly airport attire. Most people I knew dressed for comfort before getting on a plane.

"Do you really want to know what I'm reading?" I asked.

She put her hand on her hip and laughed. "You don't beat around the bush, do you?"

I shrugged. "Why? It's just a waste of time."

"I like you," she said.

"Okay." I didn't care if she liked me or not.

With her platinum-blonde hair, fake nails, and heavy makeup, she wasn't my type. Plus, the chances were high that I would never see her again.

She slinked toward me and ran a long fingernail down my arm. "You're so big."

"Yes, ma'am."

I was six feet three inches and heavily muscled, thanks to genetics and the military. Although I had retired, I kept up my daily workouts and tried to eat healthy. My knee might have taken a shit on me, but the rest of my body was still in its prime as far as I was concerned. Forty was the new thirty, and I was only thirty-eight.

"Are you big…everywhere?"

Sometimes, I liked when I got this question because I was big…everywhere. But tonight, I wasn't in the mood, so I pretended to be confused. "I don't follow, ma'am."

She laughed and pulled out the chair next to me.

Great. I should have just told her I had a tiny dick.

She leaned close to me. "You know what I mean." She leered down at my crotch so much that I wanted to cover up my lap. She looked back up at me. "Are you hung like a horse?"

Well, now, there was no way I could play dumb. "No, ma'am. Just average."

R.L. KENDERSON

She reached out to touch me, and I quickly wrapped my fingers around her wrist. If she had reached her goal before I could stop her, she'd know I was a liar, and then I'd never get rid of her.

"Please don't touch me."

She stuck out her bottom lip. "You're no fun. I just wanted to play a little. It's boring here, and I need something to do." She licked her lips.

I put her hand on her lap and let go. "Sorry, but I'm meeting a buddy soon."

"Franny, this guy bothering you?"

I groaned. I had heard the guy walk in, but I hadn't paid him any attention, as I figured he was just another flyer.

Just my luck, she had a boyfriend. How cliché.

Franny looked up and stuck out her lip. "Yes, Frank. He tried to make me touch him"—she pointed to my lap—"there."

I rolled my eyes. Now, she was playing innocent.

I turned around in my seat and looked up at the guy. He was about half a foot shorter than me, about seventy-five pounds lighter, and not the least bit intimidating. But I didn't want to get into a pissing match with him, so I stayed seated.

The guy narrowed his eyes at me. "You touched my fucking sister?"

Well, look at that. I was wrong. She was his sister.

"Technically, yes, but only to remove—"

I ducked as the brother swung at me. At the same time, I rolled my body as I'd been trained, slipping out of my seat. The guy's back was now to my front, the force of his missed swing spinning his body forty-five degrees.

"Look, I don't want to fight you. I did nothing to disrespect your sister. She came on to me, and I politely turned her down."

Frank jumped at hearing me behind him and spun to face me. "You calling my sister a slut?"

"What the fuck? No. I'm just stating facts. *Jesus Christ.*"

"He's lying," Franny yelled.

What a hypocrite.

Her brother's lips thinned into a tight line. "Do you think I'm stupid?"

I heard a beep from my carry-on.

"Excuse me," I said and walked over to open my bag.

The two siblings stared at me in shock, like they couldn't believe I was going to check my phone when we were in the middle of a fight.

And while a part of me itched to brawl, too, in the end, it wouldn't be worth it.

Mad Dog: I'll be there in five minutes.

I threw my duffel over my shoulder and turned my screen black. "Franny, Frank, it was nice meeting you both, but my ride is here."

"You can't just leave," Frank protested.

I pointed to the man behind the counter, who held a phone in his hand. "See him? He's two seconds away from calling security. Now, I don't feel like sticking around and giving a statement. Do you?"

"Yes," Franny said at the same time Frank said, "No."

I grinned and slapped Frank on the shoulder. "There you go. I don't think you're stupid at all." I spun on my heel and headed for the stairs as the two started to bicker.

Less than ten minutes later, I had my luggage, and I was getting into Maddox's SUV.

He held out his hand, and I clasped it, pulling him close.

Maddox pounded my back. "Good to see you."

We released our hands and sat back in our seats.

"You, too."

Maddox put his vehicle in drive and asked, "How's the knee?"

I squeezed it. It was a little sore after I'd dodged Frank's fist, but I thought I was going to be okay. "Great."

"Good, because we're going to be busy."

I smiled. "That sounds like heaven."

Maddox laughed. He understood where I was coming from.

"How long did it take you to get the kids to bed? You showed up earlier than I'd thought you would."

"I'm glad because it felt like forever. The baby's teething."

I grimaced. "I'll be sure to keep quiet when we get back to your place."

"About that…"

I turned my head to Maddox. "About what?"

"Addison made arrangements for you to stay in my old apartment above the accounting place."

I sent a special thank-you into the night for smart and generous women. "I can see why you married her. That was nice of her."

And she probably didn't want me bothering her kids any more than they would bother me.

Maddox snorted.

"Am I missing something?"

Maddox shook his head. "Nope. She's just not as nice as you think she is."

Whatever business Maddox had with his wife, I wasn't going to ask.

"It's all the same to me. I can go to bed when I want and wake up when I want. No crying kids. I think it's pretty nice." I grinned to myself. "Of course, now, there's no chance I'll get to accidentally see your wife naked again."

Maddox growled and reached for my shirt while I howled with laughter and swatted his fist away.

"Watch the road, dickhead."

"Don't talk about my wife naked."

"Dude, it was a joke."

Maddox huffed. "It'd better be."

I laughed again. "I missed you, man."

He eyed me out of the corner of his vision. Slowly, a smile formed across his face. "Yeah, I missed you, too."

2

OLIVIA

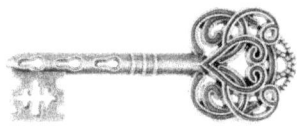

*A*s I drove into Brook Creek, I noted once again how different it was from Des Moines. I hadn't been to the small town since Addison and Maddox got married. Whenever I got together with the two of them, they came to Des Moines. I thought I had forgotten just how little their town was. It felt safer, and right now, I could use safer. My last case had taken a toll on me.

When I had started my own firm, I'd had to be there practically all the time. But we were big enough now, with enough associates and a couple of unnamed partners, that I could take a few days off. It was going to be tough for me not to call in every hour while I was gone though. Even after all I'd been through, I would never abandon my work.

Putting all that out of my mind, I walked into Addison's office, grateful for the air-conditioning. Summers were hot in Iowa.

"Hello," Addison's assistant greeted me.

I had never met her before. Maddox's niece used to work

for Addison, but now that she was close to graduating, working for Addison had gotten to be too much for Serena.

"How can I help you?"

"I'm Olivia. Addison is expecting me."

"Come back here," Addison yelled from her private office.

I chuckled. "Thanks," I told the assistant and walked back.

Addison stood from behind her desk and came around to give me a hug. "I'm so glad you came."

When we separated, I looked her up and down. "Did you doubt that I would?"

Her brown eyes lit up with a smile and a tad of guilt. "I thought maybe you were going to change your mind."

I laughed. "I did think about it once or twice, but I'm here."

"And I'm glad you are." She looked at her desk. "Do you mind if I finish up this one thing, and then I'll take you upstairs to the apartment?"

"Sure. I'll check my email while I wait."

Addison pointed to the open chairs while she took her seat back at her desk. "Sit wherever."

I sat off to the right in the corner chair to give Addison space to work and pulled out my phone.

There was a message from my assistant, Derek.

Derek: Another letter came.

I took in a deep breath, counted to five, and exhaled.

Me: What does it say?

Derek: Same as all the others.

Me: Throw it away.

Derek: Are you sure, Little Miss Don't Ever
Get Rid of Evidence?

Me: I'm sure.

Derek: Okay. You're the boss.

Me: Call me if anything else comes up.

I closed the Messages app and opened my email. I didn't want to think about Derek's texts. I had wrongly assumed that when my last case was over, the troubles that went with it would also end.

But I wasn't going to focus on that right now. I was on vacation. That stuff could wait until I got back to work.

I hoped anyway.

Turning my thoughts to something I could control, I started reading my email. I was a few in when I heard the front door open.

"Addison busy?" It was Maddox's voice.

I grinned. Even if Maddox was not the type of guy I would ever date, I really liked him and thought of him as a friend and not just the husband of a friend.

But I lost my smile when he walked in and I saw he wasn't alone.

His friend Tommy—aka Flash—was with him, and I was immediately transported back to the first time I had met him back when I was defending Maddox for assault and attempted murder.

. . .

Addison and I were in her office. Addison was behind her desk, and I was sitting in front of her with my feet up on her desk while I watched the news on my laptop. The night before, Maddox and his two friends, Thomas Morelli and Evan Malone, had rescued a mom and son from her ex-husband, who had come back to town and attacked her.

Addison and I were discussing Maddox's case and this new development when the front door opened. Addison looked up and watched through the doorway. I went back to my computer, half-listening to the conversation in the other room.

"Hey, Serena," Maddox said.

"Hey, Uncle Maddox."

"Guys, this is my niece, Serena."

"Hi," she said.

"Serena, this is Tommy, and this is Evan. I used to work with them."

"Nice to meet you," one of them said.

"The rules that apply to Addison also apply to her. Hands off." That was Maddox.

I made a noise, and Addison looked over at me.

"Please tell me I'm not representing some caveman," I said in a low voice.

Addison laughed. "Don't knock it till you try it," she whispered back. "Maddox would never boss me around…except in the bedroom." She wiggled her eyebrows. "There's something hot about being dragged off to the cave by your hair and being taken from behind."

I could feel my eyes widen, and I was sure I was looking at her like she was crazy. "No, thank you. I'll stick to nice, respectable men who treat me like a lady."

"Your orgasms must suck," a deep voice said from behind me, "and be super boring."

I jumped in my seat, and Addison almost spit out the coffee she had just taken a sip of.

I dropped my feet, turned around in my chair, and glared at the man who'd had the balls to say something like that to me. He didn't even know me.

I had to concentrate on keeping the look on my face and not showing any surprise when I saw the person who had insulted me. He was huge. Taller than an already-tall Maddox and full of muscle with dark brown hair and deep brown eyes.

I swallowed hard but retained my composure.

Piecing together the picture from the news and the info Addison had told me, I knew this guy must be Tommy.

What kind of grown man goes by Tommy?

Unfazed by my anger, he shrugged at me. "If you even have any at all. Excuse me, miss. I'd like to make you come now," *he said in a voice slightly higher than his own.* "Okay, but be careful. I can't ruin my hair or my makeup," *Tommy said, pretending to be me.*

If I were a cartoon, smoke would be coming out of my nostrils. "You don't even know me."

Tommy laughed. "I've met your kind before. Big and bad to the world, but behind closed doors, you need your ass slapped and your pussy pounded."

I gasped. This guy had some nerve.

"Flash," *Maddox said, coming into the room,* "leave my lawyer alone. I want her to defend me, not run away, cursing my name because of my friends." *He stepped around his friend.* "Please don't throw my trial because of one asshole."

Poor Maddox. He needed to invest in finding new friends.

I patted his hand. "Don't worry. I've dealt with worse men than him before." *I looked at said asshole.* "Nice name," *I said sarcastically.*

He snickered. "It's a nickname, sweetheart." *He raised his eyebrows.* "You can ask Addison about it later."

I threw my hair over my shoulder. "I don't think so."

Tommy shrugged. "Like I said, boring." He laid his head on his shoulder and pretended to snore.

Maddox socked him in the gut. "Knock it off, asswipe."

Then, he walked over to Addison's chair and lifted her out of her seat. She squealed.

He sat down in her chair and settled her on his lap. "So, what do you want to go over today?" Maddox asked and nuzzled Addison's neck.

I had to turn my eyes away as the uncomfortable feeling of jealousy filled my gut.

Thankfully, another man, who had to be Evan, walked into the office, reminding me to answer Maddox's question.

"Well, first, congratulations are in order for what happened early this morning. This will look very good to any potential jury," I said.

Tommy scowled. "Mad Dog didn't do it for the publicity. We did it because someone was in trouble."

I sighed. "I know that. But it helps our case nonetheless."

It wasn't that I didn't feel bad for the victim—because I did. A lot. It was that I was looking at the big picture. And that meant getting Maddox cleared of all charges or found not guilty in a court of law.

"She's kind of right," Evan said. "Everyone was waiting to shake Mad Dog's hand when we went to get breakfast this morning. Ours, too. But they were looking at Mad Dog like he was a hero."

Maddox scowled. "Everyone likes me now, I guess." He said something else that only Addison could hear.

She kissed him on the cheek. "You don't need them."

I went over a few more things with Maddox, and then the guys took off.

Addison went through some of her paperwork while I did some work on my computer. Unfortunately, I couldn't stop thinking about

Tommy telling me to ask Addison about his nickname. I really didn't want to know. But I did.

Damn my curiosity.

"Ask me," Addison said, not looking up from her desk.

"What?" I didn't think I had been that obvious.

She lifted her head. "I know you want to know, Olivia. Ask me."

I rolled my eyes. "How did Flash get his nickname? And what is his real name? I wasn't actually introduced." I did already know, but I didn't want to admit that I had paid attention to who he was.

"His name is Tommy. And he got the nickname because he said the ladies are gone in a flash when they go out to the bar."

"I can see why." I frowned. "He made it sound like his nickname was a good thing."

"Well, apparently, the women avoid him because they're afraid of his size."

"He is a big guy. But I didn't get the impression he'd hurt anyone."

Addison laughed. "No, not his body size. The size of his dick."

My cheeks heated.

Addison and I had met in college, but we had been more classroom friends. We hadn't hung out with the same people. None of my friends would ever say something so blunt out loud. Not that they didn't talk about sex. They just hinted about those things more and used code words.

"Oh," I said as I fingered the corner of my laptop. "That never occurred to me."

Addison chuckled. "Maybe Tommy is right, and you've been with the wrong guys. You haven't had sex until you've had sex with someone with a big cock."

My eyes widened. "Does Maddox…" The question slipped out before I could stop it.

"Hell yeah. Why do you think I can't keep my hands off him? It's big, and he knows what to do with it."

"I've never had that." Again, my mouth was speaking before my brain could stop it.

Addison grinned. "I'm sure Flash would be more than happy to show you."

I stiffened my spine. "No, thank you."

But deep inside my mind—way in the back, where no one was ever allowed—I imagined what it would be like to have sex with him. I shut that down after two seconds. Now was not the time to think about sex.

Addison gave me a once-over. "You're probably right. He might break you in two."

I shuddered at the memory. Addison had been right. I didn't know if someone my size could even handle someone as big as Tommy.

And why am I even thinking about this?

Tommy and I weren't going to sleep together.

"Ooh la la," Addison said. "Two sexy, sweaty men, walking down the street." It was clear by the clothes—or lack thereof since Tommy had opted to take his shirt off and tuck it into his shorts—and sweat that Maddox and Tommy had been doing some sort of workout, and she was right. One blond and one brunette. They looked pretty sexy together. "Did you two have to fight off all the women with a stick?"

Maddox held up his left hand and wiggled his ring finger. "They know I'm taken and I'd never stray."

"Aw," Addison said.

"Yeah, aw. But stop ogling my friend," Maddox joked.

"I'm married, not blind, Maddox," she teased back with an eyebrow wiggle.

Tommy pretended to smooth down his nonexistent shirt. I swallowed. Even from my seat off to the side, I could see he had a very nice torso with perfectly sculpted muscles.

And I didn't like it.

"Thanks for noticing, Addison. Don't worry, Mad; I'll keep your woman away from me."

"At least someone has my back," Maddox muttered.

Addison rolled her eyes and pointed to me.

Both men turned, and Maddox grinned. "Hey, Olivia. I didn't see you there."

I stood and gave him a hug. "Hey, Maddox."

After I stepped back, he pointed to Tommy. "You remember my friend Tommy, right? You met him the first time you came to Brook Creek, and he was also a guest at our wedding."

I shot Addison a quick look for not telling me that Tommy would be here. Then, I furrowed my brow as if I were confused and shook my head. "Sorry. Doesn't ring a bell."

3

TOMMY

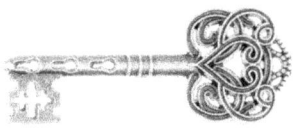

*O*livia Mayer was lying. She totally remembered who I was, or she wouldn't have said she didn't remember me and then left a minute later. If she hadn't remembered me, she would have stuck around to be introduced. Instead, she had hightailed it out of the room, telling Addison she'd meet her when she was ready.

"Addison?" Maddox said.

"Yeah?"

"Did you forget to warn Olivia that Tommy would be here?"

She shrugged. "It might have slipped my mind."

"Warn?" I butted in. "Why would you have to warn anyone I was coming?"

Addison raised her brow and looked at me like I was dense.

"Dude, you totally insulted her the first and only time you met her," Maddox said.

I tried to recall the exact conversation, but apparently, I wasn't fast enough because Mad Dog filled me in.

"You told her that her orgasms must suck."

I winced. "Oh, yeah. That." I vaguely recalled saying that to her. "I'll be back," I told Mad Dog and Addison. "Actually, I'll meet you at your place when I'm done with lunch," I added.

"Sounds good," Maddox said.

"She's probably around back," Addison called as I headed for the door.

I was grateful for the advice because Olivia wasn't out front, and the nice Lexus that had been parked there when Maddox and I first walked into the building was gone. I walked around to the back of the building to see Olivia standing next to her open trunk.

"Olivia."

She froze and slowly turned around. She crossed her arms over her chest as she bit out the word, "What?"

I came to a stop about six feet away from her. I wanted her to see my face when I apologized, but I didn't want to get too close and make her feel intimidated by my size.

Olivia was a tiny thing. While not all Asian women were short and thin, she was. I was probably over a foot taller than her and twice as wide. I would never want her to feel like she had to fear me.

"I came back here to tell you I'm sorry. The first time we met, I was incredibly rude to you. I never should have said your orgasms sucked."

She flinched.

"I'm sure you have perfectly nice orgasms," I added. "Either way, it's not my place to say."

"You're right; it's not." Her words were clipped.

Okay, so she was still mad.

I would have preferred if she'd forgiven me because her

anger was a turn-on for me. The longer she held the grudge, the more I wanted her.

And there went my dick. He was totally on board with that idea.

I clasped my hands in front of my crotch in hopes that I was blocking any view of my erection. If Olivia was mad now, she would be even more pissed if she saw that I was hard.

"I know there is no excuse for what I said, but I was a weird combination of high on adrenaline and tired from lack of sleep. I was hoping we could start over."

She narrowed her brown eyes at me. "I'll think about it."

I clenched my jaw and tried not to say something that would get me in more trouble. I might have been telling the truth about why I'd said those things to Olivia the first time I met her, but I'd left out the part where I was generally a blunt person, no matter what. Would I have said those things if I hadn't helped Maddox rescue a local townswoman and her son in the middle of the night? The answer was maybe because I couldn't know for sure that I would have kept my mouth shut.

I counted to ten and took a deep breath. "Fair enough. You just let me know when you've decided." I nodded and headed next door.

"Where are you going?" she yelled when I almost reached my door.

I stopped and turned. "To my place to find some lunch."

Her eyes widened. "Aren't you staying with Addison and Maddox?"

I couldn't help the smile that spread across my face. "Nope. And if you're staying in Addison's old place, it looks like you and I are going to be neighbors."

She seemed to think about this and then slowly walked over to me. "Okay."

I stared at her, waiting for her to say more.

"Okay what?"

"Okay, we can start over."

"Just like that, huh?"

She chuckled and shrugged. "Yeah. Why not? I'm going to be here a week, and I really don't want to waste the energy being mad at someone." She tilted her head to the side. "Unless you're leaving tomorrow or soon after."

I laughed. "Sorry, sweetheart, I'm here for a month, and I just arrived two days ago."

"I guess it's a truce then."

I held out my hand, and when she shook it, I said, "Truce."

She pulled her arm away. "Don't call me sweetheart though."

"Deal."

She turned to walk back to her car.

"But…"

She paused and turned halfway. "But what?"

I walked over to her and leaned down next to her ear.

I waited a beat to see if she would push me away, but when I heard her suck in a breath, I knew I was good to answer her question.

"But if you ever need someone to slap your ass and pound your pussy, making sure you have an orgasm that doesn't suck, hit me up. I haven't had a good, long fuck in a while." I slapped her butt and walked away, leaving her standing there, mouth hanging open with plenty to think about.

4

OLIVIA

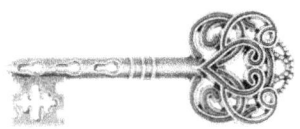

"*O*livia?"

    I spun around as Addison came up behind me.

"What are you doing?" she asked.

Standing here, waiting for the shock to wear off.

I shook my head. "Nothing. I was just talking to Tommy," I said as I rubbed my bottom.

Tommy's slap hadn't actually hurt, but I could still feel the effects. And I wasn't sure how I felt about that.

Addison wrung her hands together. "Oh? And what did he have to say?"

That he wants to have sex with me.

Holy shit.

I couldn't believe he'd said that. So blunt and forward.

I shook my head to clear it because that was not what Addison was asking about.

I put my hands on my hips. "Why didn't you tell me he was going to be here?"

She smiled awkwardly. "Because then you wouldn't have come."

"You're right about that."

The last time I'd seen him, at the wedding, I had made sure to avoid him all night. Thankfully, Addison and Maddox had had plenty of guests, making it easy for me to stay away from him.

She put her hands up in front of her and stepped closer. "Look, we don't have to hang out with the guys at all, if you really don't want to."

That meant Addison would spend less time with her husband, and I wasn't going to do that to her. Especially when they had two kids together. I didn't know how that would even work.

"No, it's fine. He actually apologized to me."

She smiled. "He did?" She cleared her throat. "I mean, of course he did. Maddox has good friends."

I laughed and rolled my eyes. *Do good friends hit on their friend's wife's friend?*

"But seriously, did you invite me here when you knew Tommy was going to be here?"

"Well…"

I had thought she would say no right away. "Why?"

"Because…" She bit her lip.

"Because why, Addison?"

"Because you need to get laid. Remember we talked about this? And I know every guy in town, and none of them are right for you."

My eyebrows shot up. "And you think Tommy the Flash is?"

"It's just Flash, no *the*. And he might not be right for you as a boyfriend." She stepped closer and lowered her voice. "But he's the perfect rebound guy. He's the type who can fuck you into a coma and make you forget all about Ray and anything else bothering you. Then, you can go back to Des Moines with a whole new outlook."

I wrinkled my nose. "And you think sex is going to do that for me?"

"No. *Great* sex is going to do that for you."

"And how do you know that Tommy is even capable of having great sex?"

She smirked. "Because he's just like Maddox. He's a former Navy SEAL, so he has total command over his body. He's confident, and guessing by what he said to you the first time you met him, he's good at dirty talk." She whispered, "Don't tell Maddox, but even I got a little turned on when he said that you needed to be spanked and fucked hard."

I swallowed. "Those weren't his exact words."

Addison's eyes widened, and her face lit up in a grin. "Oh my God, you remember what he said to you."

"Of course I remember. I'd never been so insulted in my life."

She laughed. "Insulted…*and* a little curious." She lifted up a finger. "And don't you say you weren't."

"Okay. *Maybe* I was a little curious." *Was and still am.*

Addison wiggled her eyebrows.

"I said, maybe."

Knowing when not to push something, Addison changed the subject. "Come on. I'll show you around upstairs."

She helped me grab my things from my trunk, and we walked up the sturdy but creaky staircase to the apartment above her office.

She unlocked the dead bolt and handed me the key. "It's not big, but you won't be here long."

"I remember from when I was here last time." I grabbed on to the door and shook it to test how sturdy it was. Even with a dead bolt, doors could be broken.

She set my stuff down by the door. "I left a lot of things here when Maddox and I bought our own place." She pointed toward the kitchen. "There are dishes in the cupboard, and I put some essentials in the fridge. You'll probably have to go shopping though."

"I'll do that this afternoon while you're at work."

She pointed to the couch. "I left the couch, but I took my TV. But I assume you have your laptop in case you want to watch anything."

"TV? What's that?" I joked and patted the bag hanging on my shoulder. "My computer is right here. And I'm fine without a television. I barely have time to watch anything other than the news I turn on while I'm getting ready in the morning."

"Tell me about it." She gestured toward the bathroom. "I put clean towels in the bathroom along with the basic toiletries. I figured you'd probably bring a lot of your own stuff."

I nodded.

She turned her attention to the bedroom. "I left my bed and all my bedroom furniture when I moved. Maddox insisted we get a king-size bed, and mine is only a queen. I was going to eventually bring it over for a guest room, but then both boys were born, and we ran out of bedrooms. So, here it stays." She put her hand on my arm. "I put on fresh sheets this morning."

"Thank you."

I set my laptop bag down on her kitchen table and turned

around. I pointed to the wall behind me. "I don't remember that window being there."

Addison looked. "Oh, I used to have a big bookcase in front of the window because it has a direct line of sight into that room, where Tommy is staying. These buildings were built very close together, so I put the bookcase there when I first moved in because I didn't want my previous neighbors looking in and catching me naked or something. The bookcase was there so long that I forgot about the window until I moved the bookcase to the new house." She tapped her chin and said to herself, "Why didn't I remember that when Maddox moved in? I could have spied on him."

"Addison."

"What?"

"You can't spy on someone even if he is now your husband."

She rolled her eyes. "I was kidding."

"No, you weren't."

She laughed. "You're right. I wasn't." She walked over to the small pane of glass. "You honestly can't see much anyway, but you still might want to put up a towel or something."

I walked up behind her. I could barely make out furniture in the apartment next door, to the point that I wasn't even sure what I was looking at. "I'm sure I'll be fine."

Addison turned around. "I'll leave, so you can get situated." She looked at her watch. "We're grilling out at our house for dinner, so you should have plenty of time to unpack and go to the store."

"What time should I come over?"

"Maddox will probably pick the boys up from daycare at five, so around then."

"I'll be there."

She put her hand on my arm. "But no earlier, okay?"

I laughed. "Okay." I liked being early to everything.

"I'm serious," she said with a smile because she knew I was always punctual.

I put an X over my heart. "I promise."

5

TOMMY

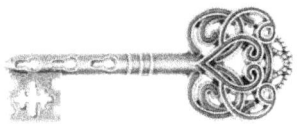

After lunch, I walked over to Maddox and Addison's place because their town was that small. It took me a good twenty minutes, but it wasn't worth having Maddox come and pick me up.

When I got there, I walked around to the backyard and pulled out my earbuds. When Maddox had said he was keeping me busy while I was in town, he'd meant it. His house was old, and while he had already updated a lot of things upstairs, his basement still gave off a dungeon vibe with half of it unfinished. Before we started on the inside though, we were going to make the tiny windows into full-sized ones, so they would bring in more light. We would also make them big enough that someone could crawl out of them if there was a fire.

Maddox looked up from his work and rested his arm on the shovel he'd just been using. "Hey, Addison told me you apologized to Olivia."

I shrugged. "Yeah. It was the right thing to do."

I waited for him to add that I had come on to her and canceled out any apology I had given.

"Thanks. It was going to be a long week if you and Olivia were butting heads the whole time. It makes things easier on Addison and me."

Interesting. So, Olivia hadn't told Addison that I'd offered to have sex with her.

Or Addison hadn't told Maddox that.

Nah. Addison totally would have told her husband. Those two hardly kept anything from each other.

Which meant I needed to file this information away for later.

"It's the least I could do. I was pretty rude to her. I don't know what came over me."

Maddox laughed. "I do."

I picked up the other shovel. "Oh, yeah? And what's that?"

He wiped off a bead of sweat from his forehead. "You were just being you. You always speak your mind. It's one of the things I like about you."

"Yeah, it worked well when we were active duty." When we had been out in the field, there hadn't been time to tiptoe around things. When issues arose, they needed to be dealt with immediately. "But being a civilian now, I might need to reevaluate the things I say." Maybe my nickname was Flash because I made people disappear by being so blunt.

"Nah," Maddox said. "Now, help me dig, so we can put in the new windows tomorrow."

I put in my earbuds, turned on my music, and went to work.

———

After a couple hours, Maddox approached me, so I hit pause on my phone and took an earbud out so that I could hear him better.

"Hey, Addy is going to be home soon, and I have to pick up the boys from daycare, so we should probably call it quits."

I looked at my watch and furrowed my brow. "It's only three in the afternoon. Don't you usually pick the kids up at five or something?"

"Yes, but I need to shower and also get ready for dinner since everyone is coming over tonight."

I still didn't understand why he needed that much time to get ready. "Do you need any help?"

"Maybe later, but Addison and I have it handled for right now."

I studied my friend. We'd worked together a long time, and I could tell when something was up. "So, you and Addison are going to be making dinner, huh?"

"Yes."

"That's what we're calling sex these days?"

Maddox shook his head and threw his hands up. "Yes, my wife is coming home a couple hours early, so I can fuck her, okay? You and I have been busy working on the house, she's been preparing for Olivia's arrival, and the boys make it really hard to get more than a quickie in."

I started laughing. "Dude, you don't have to justify having sex with your wife to me. If I had a wife"—I was going to add *like Addison* until Maddox narrowed his eyes, so I left that part off—"I would want to have sex with her, too. I mean, why else have a wife?"

Maddox snorted. "That's why you don't have a wife. They are not your personal sex worker."

I raised my eyebrows. "Sex worker?"

"My lovely wife has been keeping me on the up and up and says that I spend too much time in an all-male environment. She said that if I'm going to work in law enforcement, I need to eliminate sexist ideas that many police officers practice. One of those is to stop calling women who work in the sex industry prostitutes and hookers. *Sex worker* recognizes that that they are workers, and it loses some of the negativity that is associated with the other titles."

"Wow. That was more of an explanation than I needed."

He shrugged. "You asked."

"You're right; I did. And while I'm glad your wife is educating you, I could have gone with the CliffsNotes version."

I was happy that Maddox was liking his new career and was actually trying to be a good sheriff, unlike the previous guy. But jealousy turned in my gut. I'd retired from the Navy four months ago, and I still didn't know what I wanted to do with the rest of my life. I tried to blame some of my waiting on my knee surgery, but I was just putting off the inevitable. I was going to have to find a job.

First, I'd have to find a place to live. I still lived in my house in Virginia, but being away from there, even for only a few days, had made me realize I couldn't stay there and not feel homesick for the SEALs. And I didn't want to return to New York, where I'd grown up. I'd never loved it there, which was one of the reasons I'd joined the military.

At the moment, I felt pretty lost, and I didn't like it.

"Everything okay?" Maddox asked.

I smiled. "Yeah. But I'd better get going. What time should I be back for dinner? Do I need to bring anything?"

"I'll pick the boys up around five, so a little after. Addison will be here if I'm not back yet."

"Okay. I'll see you then," I said. I put my earbud back in, hit play on my phone, and headed back to the apartment.

6

OLIVIA

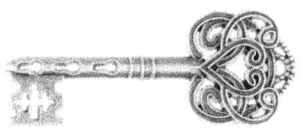

I pulled up to Addison and Maddox's house at twenty minutes to five.

I had already done my grocery shopping and unpacked. Since it was almost five o'clock anyway, I had decided to head over to her house.

I had only been there once before, but it looked the same as I remembered.

Maddox's SUV was in the garage along with Addison's minivan. In the driveway was Maddox's work vehicle—an SUV that read *Carford County Sheriff* on the side.

As I walked up the driveway, I had to wonder if the block had coordinated their lawn mowing to be on the same day. The neighbor right next door and the neighbor across the street were mowing, and then another guy a few houses up was also cutting his yard.

With the garage door open, I decided to enter the house that way since the front door was more formal. Once I was in the garage, I could see through the screen door that the main door was only about three-fourths of the way closed. I was surprised because it was so hot outside. But Addison must have left it open because she knew I was coming over.

While I was sure Addison wouldn't care if I simply walked into her house, I knocked on the screen door anyway. I heard what sounded like a voice call out, but I couldn't be sure because at the same time, the next-door neighbor chose that moment to mow the edge of his yard, right next to the garage.

But my friend knew I was coming, so I figured she was calling me in. It felt silly to yell back into the house and ask if she had told me to come in when I could just walk inside.

But within moments of entering the house, I realized Addison had not been yelling for me to enter. And I also knew why she hadn't wanted me to come early. And more importantly, I understood that I should have listened to her.

Addison and Maddox were having sex in the living room, and it was not like any sex that I'd had before.

They looked like something I'd see on-screen. But not porn, where everything was for the cameras and the woman was faking it. This was like in an R-rated movie or a TV-MA show.

Maddox pushed Addison's dark hair out of the way as he pounded into her. It wasn't a word I would normally use to describe sex, but there was nothing else as accurate. Her knees were up by her waist like she wanted him in as deeply as he could go.

Addison reached up, and I thought she was going to wrap her hand around the back of Maddox's neck, but she changed direction and pushed her hand against the back of her couch, as if she was bracing herself.

No *as if*. The way Maddox was screwing her, she was definitely bracing herself.

Maddox threaded his fingers through Addison's hair with one hand and cupped the side of her head with the other.

"Are you going to come?" he asked her.

She made a low, "Mmhmm," noise in response that sounded like she was in pain…or at the height of pleasure.

Maddox stared into his wife's eyes, as if he was waiting for something, and when she came, I knew that was what he had been holding out for. He shoved his hips into Addison's as he climaxed, looking in her eyes the whole time.

I felt like a total perv for standing there and watching them. It was such an intimate moment.

But when Maddox kissed Addison as they lay there, connected, I realized that was more intimate than anything.

I needed to get out of there.

Thankfully, I heard the lawn mower move closer to the house, and I used the noise to cover up my escape.

I made it around to the front of the house and collapsed on the steps of the porch. My legs were like gelatin from the adrenaline rush of almost getting caught.

Yet my skin felt like it was on fire, and when I opened my legs under my summer dress to catch a breeze, I realized my underwear was soaked. I looked down at myself to see my nipples poking through my dress and my bra.

I'd had a handful of boyfriends in my life, and I didn't think I'd ever been as turned on as I was at that moment.

I pulled my legs closer and rested my head on my knees.

I needed to do some deep breathing and focus my thoughts on something else.

"You okay?"

I jumped and screeched. I flung my head up to see Tommy standing in front of me, but I quickly lowered my eyes before he could read my face. I was sure *voyeur* was written all over it.

But that wasn't the smartest move because my eyes landed on his crotch, and even though he wasn't hard, I could still see the outline of his dick through his shorts. I was getting wet again.

I groaned and dropped my head back to my knees.

I sensed Tommy taking a seat beside me. "That bad, huh?"

"I don't even know what to say," I said into my legs.

"Okay, let's start with something easy. Why are you sitting out here?"

"I arrived too early."

"That doesn't seem so bad. I'm a little early, too."

"I…" I couldn't believe I was going to tell him this, but it was like I needed someone to share my pain. "I walked into the house, and I shouldn't have. I saw —"

Tommy burst out laughing, so I sat up.

He had his hand on his chest, as if he couldn't breathe from laughing so hard.

"What's so funny?" I hadn't even told him what I'd seen.

"You saw Maddox and Addison having sex."

I narrowed my eyes. "How did you know?"

"Because when I was here earlier, Maddox told me to leave, so he could fuck his wife."

"Yeah, well, Addison didn't warn me." I wrinkled my nose. "And do you have to be so crude?"

Tommy laughed again. "Those were his words, not mine." He leaned close to my ear. "And there is nothing wrong with the word *fuck*."

I shivered. "Agree to disagree."

"I've never met someone who needs it more."

43

I swung my head around to glare at him. "I've been…*you know*."

"Honey, I don't want to start another fight with you, but if you've been…*you know*…you wouldn't be sitting out here, so shaken up about what you just saw or about me saying the very word."

He lifted my leg over his knee. He put his hand on my ankle and slowly ran it up toward my crotch. I watched it slip under the dress, as if I were in someone else's body. He reached the top of my thigh and cupped me between the legs.

"So hot." He removed his hand and set my foot on the step. "Like I said, I've never met someone who needs it more."

It took me a second to find my voice. "And how do you know that?"

"Because you didn't stop me from touching you." He leaned closer again. "And you probably didn't realize it, but you spread your legs for me just a tiny bit further."

I wanted to argue more—I was a professional at arguing after all—but this was a disagreement I wasn't going to win. And I was smart enough to know when to back down before I lost.

As luck would have it, Addison and Maddox came outside from the garage at that moment. I was saved from having to concede to Tommy.

"Hey, Maddison," Tommy said.

"Maddison?" I asked.

"It's their couple name," he said and stood as I stared at him

He was an odd duck. One minute, he was saying *fuck* to me, and then another, he was giving our friends a couple name.

7

TOMMY

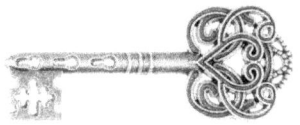

"I'll be right back," Maddox said and kissed his wife on the cheek. He looked at me. "You want to go with me to pick up the boys?"

I loved his boys, but I was more interested in watching Olivia try not to be embarrassed around Addison. "Nah, I'll stay here."

"Beer's in the fridge," he said to me before he hopped in the minivan and took off.

At the same moment, I heard Olivia come up behind me.

"How long have you been here?" Addison asked us.

"A few minutes," I said before Olivia could answer.

Addison smiled at her friend. "Hey, you listened to me for once about not coming early." She turned around as Olivia made a choking noise. "Come inside. I'll pour us some wine."

I didn't immediately follow because I was trying to hold in a laugh, and I didn't want Addison to notice. Olivia did though, and she elbowed me in the gut as she walked by.

"Oof." I rubbed my abdomen as I trailed behind the two women. Olivia was stronger than she looked.

In the kitchen, Addison pulled a beer from the fridge for me and grabbed wine and wineglasses for her and Olivia.

I didn't know if Addison could sense the weird tension in the room, but I could, so I decided to step in. "Who's all coming tonight?"

"You and Olivia, obviously. Also, Maddox's mom, brother, sister, and niece."

"That'll be nice."

Addison slid a glass over to Olivia, who picked it up and downed the whole thing.

Addison's eyebrows flew up practically to her hairline. "Everything okay?"

"Hmm?" Olivia said.

She glanced at me, but there was no way I could tell her she needed to chill out without Addison noticing, so I purposely eyed her empty wineglass in hopes that she would get the message.

"Oh," Olivia said. "Yeah, everything's fine."

She smiled awkwardly, and I tried not to cringe.

Addison filled up Olivia's glass with more wine. "Do you want to go and sit in the living room or in the backyard? It's shaded out there, so it's not too hot."

Olivia almost spit out the sip of wine she'd just taken. "*Outside.*"

Addison laughed. "I didn't think you'd care so much. Outside it is," she said as she walked to the sliding glass doors.

Once she was out of earshot, I leaned over and whispered to Olivia, "Get it together. If you can stand up in a courtroom with criminals and judges, you can talk to your friend. Besides, sex is natural. Everyone has it."

I could be mistaken, but I thought I saw a shiver.

"You're right. I just can't stop…picturing it."

"And it's turning you on?"

She whipped her head around. "*No.*"

I grinned. "Liar."

I stepped around her and went outside to join Addison. I took a seat across from her at the round patio table so that Olivia and Maddox could sit on either side of her.

Olivia walked out with her head held high and sat down between Addison and me. But she made sure to shoot me a dirty look.

I took a big swig of my beer. "You're right. It's not too hot out here. But for some reason, Olivia's face is already red. Maybe you should put on sunblock."

Anger flared behind her eyes, and I was pretty sure she wanted me dead, but I didn't care. I was having too much fun.

"Tommy's right. Your face is a little pink."

"I'll be fine," Olivia said with a forced smile.

There was a commotion from the house, and Addison turned to see her husband and kids. "I'd better go help Maddox."

The second she walked away, Olivia kicked me under the table.

I laughed and shook my head. "You'll have to try harder than that if you want to hurt me."

She elbowed me once more.

I laughed again.

She narrowed her eyes before she reached under the table, and I felt pressure on my leg.

"Did you just pinch me?"

Her jaw tightened. "*Grr.* Doesn't anything hurt you?"

47

I grinned. "Nope." I frowned. "I mean, besides the obvious. I am a man."

Olivia's eyes sparkled, and just as her arm swung out toward my crotch, all four Wolfes came outside.

Thankfully, I was fast, and I caught her hand before it collided with my junk. But since I was afraid she'd do it again, I clamped my hand down on hers, trapping it between my palm and my upper thigh.

"Hey, Spencer. Hey, Thane," I said as Olivia tried to pull her hand away. I increased my hold.

Thane smiled at me, and drool slid over his cute little chin.

"Tommy," Spencer said and rushed over to me.

I reluctantly let go of Olivia.

"*Yook*," Spencer said. "Car." He held up a Hot Wheels toy.

"Cool. Can I see it?"

"No."

"*Spencer*," Addison said, but I laughed.

"It's okay."

"Spence, go play, buddy," Maddox said, and Spencer ran to the sandbox out in his yard.

"Let me see Thane," I said, holding out my arms.

Maddox handed him to me as he sat down beside me.

"Hey, buddy."

I got another smile and more drool.

"What are you men doing out here?" Olivia asked as she peered at the yard and the work Maddox and I had been doing there.

"Tommy and I are putting in egress windows, and then we're going to redo the basement. We're hoping to put a family room down there along with another bedroom and bathroom, so guests have somewhere to stay."

"That sounds like a lot of work."

Maddox shrugged. "I already did our bedroom and the kitchen. It *is* a lot of work, but it'll be worth it when it's done."

I set Thane's butt on the table, so he could face me. "Except no one wants to stay at your mommy and daddy's house," I said in a baby voice. "No, no, no. Mommy and Daddy have too much sex, and their room is going to be right above the new guest room. Mommy and Daddy had better buy earplugs."

Thane giggled as if he actually knew what I was talking about.

Maddox and Addison were rolling their eyes, but Olivia looked horrified.

I made a face at Thane because I had gotten the exact reaction out of her that I was looking for.

"Quit talking to my six-month-old about sex, Tommy," Addison said. "And if you stayed in our guest room, we would be sure not to do anything while you were there."

"Speak for yourself," Maddox protested.

"Oh, I'm fine with you two"—I looked at Thane—"having relations while I'm in the house. It's someone else who can't handle it." I nodded my head rather enthusiastically toward Olivia.

She gasped and stomped her heel on my insole.

"*Mother...fudger,*" I said just in time before I accidentally swore in front of the baby.

Thane laughed at me, as did Mad Dog and Addison, while Olivia smiled smugly.

"That hurt," I said through clenched teeth.

"Good," she said and took a drink of her wine.

8

OLIVIA

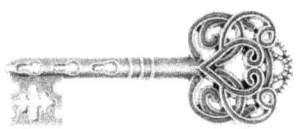

"*H*ey, Tommy, would you mind going to Des Moines tomorrow to pick up the windows? You can take my SUV. I need to do a few things at the station for work, and then I can finish up here, so we can install them when you get back."

My ears perked up at the mention of Des Moines. "I'll go with you to help."

Three pairs of eyes turned to me.

"No way," Addison said.

"Why not?"

She narrowed her eyes. "Because you just want to check in at work. You only got here today."

"But, I mean, if Tommy is going anyway, like I said, I can help."

Tommy laughed. "The store will bring the windows right to my vehicle. I don't need help. Besides, you couldn't lift one even if you did really want to help."

"I'm stronger than I look."

"You can go if you apologize for stepping on my foot."

I started to protest that he had goaded me first, but it was pointless. "Fine. I'm sorry."

He shrugged. "Whatever. I don't care if you come with. You can keep me company."

"Why, you..."

He'd tricked me.

"Focus on what's important," he said to me.

He had a point.

I turned and smiled triumphantly to Addison. "See, Tommy doesn't care if I come with."

She stuck out her bottom lip. "But I thought you came to hang out with me."

"But I thought you had to help someone with a will tomorrow?" Maddox asked her.

Addison glared at her husband.

He laughed. "Sorry, babe."

She sighed and looked at Tommy. "Olivia can go with you, but I'm warning you. She's going to try and get you to take her to work. And when she does, she only gets a half hour, tops. If you give her more than that, she'll never leave. And if she refuses, I give you permission to pick her up and carry her out of there."

"Hey, I'm right here. And since when did you become the boss of me?" I said with a pout.

"Since you don't know how to relax and take a vacation," Addison retorted.

I crossed my arms across my chest. I didn't like being treated like a child, but she wasn't wrong.

"I can do that," Tommy said. "I'll carry her out of there if I have to."

Addison laughed. "I'd love to see that."

———

"I know it's not as exciting as work, but did you have a good time?"

Addison handed me a dish, and I put it in the dishwasher. All the other guests had gone home, the kids were asleep in bed, and Tommy and Maddox were still outside, so the two of us were alone in the kitchen.

"Yes. It was fun and relaxing. I forget how nice it is not to worry about work all the time," I admitted. Or the things that came along with being a defense attorney.

"Is everything okay on that front? I know you won that big case."

I smiled. "I did win. And it felt really good." What came after, not so much. But I didn't want to bother her with that stuff. "I know I need some time off like this, but it's hard to let go every now and then. My firm is my baby." And with no husband and kids, sometimes, it felt like it was my family.

Addison put her hand on my shoulder. "I understand. Until Maddox came back, my work was my baby. And I'm just a one-man show. You and your partners built up your firm from the three of you to what it is now. I can see why you put a lot of energy into it. But remember, you hired all those people because they are competent. If you don't think they can manage without you, you wouldn't have brought them on."

I chuckled. "You have a way with words. Maybe you and Maddox should move to Des Moines, and you can join my team. We could use someone like you in court."

She scrunched up her nose. "Nah. I like my little life here." She rinsed off a glass and handed it to me. "Which is so crazy when I think about it. Maddox and I had such grand plans to get out of this town and do bigger and better things. And now, here we are…happy."

"Life is funny sometimes."

We cleaned up a few more dishes in silence before Addison said, "So…"

"So…what?" I asked. I had no idea what she was thinking.

"So, you want to tell me why you were acting so strange earlier tonight?"

I winced. "You noticed, huh?"

She laughed. "Of course I noticed. Tommy didn't exactly help. He kept watching you."

A hot flash went through my body. "He did?" I asked more eagerly than I should have.

"Yeah, he was watching you like he was waiting for you to mess up or something."

"Oh." I wasn't prepared for the disappointment that followed.

A slow grin spread across Addison's face. "Did you want him to be watching you for other reasons?"

"What?" I scoffed. "No."

"Because when your attention is elsewhere, he looks at you like he wants to do things to you. Very bad things." She wiggled her eyebrows.

I shook my head, even as I tried not to let any excitement get the best of me. "No, he doesn't."

"Yes, he does. But we're getting off topic. Why were you being weird?"

I didn't know what to do. I could make something up, but then I'd be lying. Or I could tell her the truth and potentially embarrass her. Or worse, she could get mad at me for not listening to her.

Thanks to the help of a few glasses of wine, I decided to go with the truth.

"I got here early even though you told me not to, the door to the garage was open partway, I walked into your house, and I saw you and Maddox having porn-star sex. Like, *porn-star* sex," I blurted out before I could change my mind.

Addison's eyes rounded to the size of the plate she was holding. She stared at me; the only movement she made was when she blinked.

I bit my lip. "I'm sorry. Are you—"

She leaned close. "Was it hot? What did I look like? Did I look stupid?"

"Uh…" This was not the reaction I'd expected from her.

"I've always wanted to record Maddox and me having sex, but I'm worried that seeing myself will ruin it because I'll be too busy judging my flaws and technique."

It was my turn to stare at her.

"Come on, Olivia. Don't leave me hanging."

I tilted my head. "So, you're not mad?"

"Not really. I should have known you wouldn't listen to me. And next time, instead of telling Maddox to make sure the door is locked, I'm going to lock it myself."

"Okay then…yes…it was hot. But also weird because you're my friends."

"I can understand that."

"And there was one other thing."

"What's that?"

"I was jealous. I've *never* had sex like that," I confessed.

"Never had sex like what?" a deep voice asked from the direction of the sliding doors.

Addison and I both jumped and then turned to see who had snuck into the house without us hearing a single thing.

Tommy and Maddox both stood there with a beer in their hands. I studied their faces to see if I could guess how much they'd heard. I also couldn't tell which one of them had asked the question. They had surprisingly neutral expressions.

"How long have you been standing there?" I asked.

"How did we not hear you come in?" Addison asked.

The two men looked at each other and clinked their beer bottles together.

"Baby, I've told you, we're SEALs," Maddox said. He set his beer down on the counter, came up behind Addison, and wrapped his arms around her. "We're stealthy, and we know how to get into *secret* places." He pushed her brown hair off her shoulder and kissed her neck.

There was that feeling of envy again. It was time to go.

Addison laughed and tried to shake him off. "Maddox, I'm busy, talking to my friend."

I grabbed the dish out of her hand and plopped it into the dishwasher. "That's okay. I should go and get some sleep anyway."

She put her head on her husband's shoulder and looked at him. "You scared away my helper. Now, you have to finish doing the dishes with me."

He released his wife and stepped back before turning to me. "Don't go, Olivia. Addison needs your help."

I shook my head with a laugh. "Too late," I said as I went and picked up my purse and pulled out my keys.

"I'd better get going, too," Tommy said. "Olivia and I are going to head out early in the morning."

Since when? "We are?"

"Yep, we are."

"Okay." That was fine by me.

Tommy plucked my keys out of my hand and set them on

the counter. "Olivia and I will pick up your SUV and her car tomorrow."

I made a sound of protest. "Why'd you do that?"

"Because we've both been drinking." He put his hand on my shoulder. "Come on. I'll walk you home."

9

TOMMY

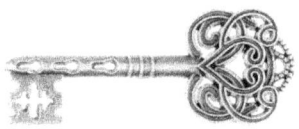

*J*directed Olivia out the door, and once it closed behind us, she said, "I can drive. I'm not drunk."

"It doesn't mean you're under the legal limit, and you literally just left the county sheriff's house. Besides, it's a beautiful night, and we don't have that far to walk."

Now that the sun had set, the temperature was perfect—not too hot and not too cold.

"But what about getting up early? If we drove, we could be in bed sooner."

I immediately pictured us in bed…together. But that wasn't what she meant.

"I just said that to get us out of there. You looked uncomfortable around Maddison's PDA."

She glanced at me and smiled. "Thanks, but no, I wasn't uncomfortable. Jealous maybe but not uncomfortable." She rolled her eyes and laughed. "Sorry. I might not be drunk, but the wine is bringing out the honesty in me tonight."

"No apologies needed. I think everyone gets lonely sometimes."

"Even you?"

"Sure, even me." More so now that I didn't have my career to keep me busy.

We walked a few minutes, just enjoying the night while I tried not to keep glancing at her. She was cute tonight, all relaxed after an evening with friends. The alcohol probably didn't hurt either.

"I have a question," Olivia said.

"Okay."

"How long were you and Maddox standing there when you came in from the backyard? How much did you hear? Or I guess, how much did Maddox hear? I'm going to be so embarrassed if he knows that I saw him having sex."

"Only for a few seconds."

She put her hand to her chest. "Whew."

"But it doesn't matter. He already knows."

Olivia smacked my arm, stopping me. She turned to face me. "How the hell does he know? Did he see me watching?" She slapped her cheeks. "Oh my God, I can never face him again."

"He didn't see you."

She dropped her arms. "Oh, thank God." Her eyes narrowed at me. "So then, how does he know?"

I brought my hands up in surrender. "I didn't tell him."

"Then, he doesn't know." She shook her head at me and started walking again.

"You do know he's married, right? Addison tells him everything."

She clenched her fists. "Shit. You're right." She took a deep breath and exhaled. "I guess that means, tomorrow, I'm driving myself back to Des Moines and never coming back."

I laughed at her. "It's not that bad." I lifted a shoulder.

"Besides, I know Maddox, and he's not going to care if you saw him."

"You can't possibly know that," she said, her voice full of skepticism.

"The dude has had sex while I was in the same room on multiple occasions, and vice versa. He's even had sex when I was in the same bed."

Her eyes bugged out at me.

"Not *with* me. Christ. Not that there's anything wrong with that. It's just not Maddox's jam. Or mine." I liked women way too much.

"Didn't that bother you?"

"That he had sex while I was trying to sleep?"

"Yeah."

"Yes. I was trying to sleep. He kept me up." I smiled. "Also, he was getting some, and I wasn't. It didn't seem fair."

"Was it…" Olivia cleared her throat. "Was it with Addison?"

I laughed. "No way. Maddox would never do that with Addison. He loves that woman too much and is too possessive."

"Then, how do you know he won't be mad that I saw him?"

Olivia had a point, but…

"You're a woman, and I'm a guy. He doesn't want other men seeing his wife naked." Especially since it had already happened once.

The first time I had visited Brook Creek, Addison had been half-asleep when she walked out of Maddox's room without anything on but her birthday suit. I wasn't one to ogle another guy's woman, but let's just say, I could under-stand why Maddox was protective.

As we walked, I noticed that Olivia had moved closer to me. We were going past the town's school, where the streetlights were few and far between. Sometimes, as a big guy with lots of training, I forgot how scared women could get.

My suspicions were confirmed when we heard a noise coming from the field behind the school, and she grabbed on to me and glued herself to my side.

Two seconds later, a cat ran out from the field and across the road.

I couldn't help but laugh. "Look, it's just a cat," I said to reassure her, but she was still watching the darkness of the field, and I could feel her body trembling.

I wrapped my arm around her.

"Hey, hey." I rubbed my hand up and down her arm. "You okay?"

She was really scared.

"Let's keep walking, okay?" Her fingers gripped me tighter.

"Don't worry. I won't let go." I gave her body a little nudge. "Come on. We're almost there." We were only about halfway, but I wasn't going to tell her that.

We continued on, close like that, but once we were around homes again and more lighting, Olivia's hold on me loosened.

"The day is ending a lot differently than it started."

"What do you mean?" she asked me.

"This morning, you hated my guts, and now, you can't keep your hands off me."

She jumped back as if I'd stuck a hot poker in her side, as if she'd just realized that she was clutching on to me.

She cleared her throat. "Yeah, well, I didn't really hate you."

I raised my eyebrows. "You sure about that?"

"I would say I had a strong aversion to you. Hate sounds too mean."

"That's good to know."

"But you apologized, and sometimes, I feel like a third wheel with Addison and Maddox. Who else can sympathize but you?"

I nodded in agreement.

Soon, we arrived at our buildings.

"Do you want me to walk you up?" The door into the building wasn't locked, and seeing as how she had been skittish earlier, I thought I'd ask.

She hesitated before saying, "I'll be fine."

I opened the door. "Go on. I'll be right behind you."

Her lips parted.

I smiled. "Just go, Olivia," I said before she could argue.

She listened this time. We climbed the rickety steps, and I watched her unlock the door, listening for the sound of the dead bolt opening.

"Do you want me to check inside before you go in?"

"No. I was just being silly earlier." She put her hand on my chest. "Thank you though. I appreciate the offer."

I looked down. It felt like she was burning a hole through my skin. I stared up into her brown eyes. "I won't go in on one condition."

"Okay, what's that?"

"Tell me the truth. What did you mean when you said you'd never had sex like that?"

10

OLIVIA

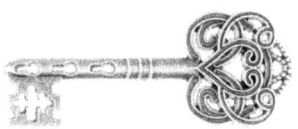

I had already admitted too many things tonight and had that embarrassing moment where I got scared. Nobody was going to hurt me here.

But I was not going to tell Tommy—the guy who had told me I needed my ass slapped and my pussy pounded—that I had never had amazing sex. Good sex? Sure. But on a scale of one to ten, I'd probably rate the best sex I'd had at a five.

Until tonight, I had thought rated-ten sex was only something you saw on TV or read about.

And now, I was getting wet, just thinking about it again.

I was so ashamed. They were my *friends*.

Tommy put his hand on mine, and that was when I realized I was still touching him.

I quickly pulled away, and he lifted a brow.

"Go ahead. Check the apartment."

Disappointment flashed across his face, but he didn't say anything. And I waited by the door for him to do his sweep so that I could regain some more composure.

He was back in less than five minutes. "All clear."

"Shocking," I said.

He laughed. "You can deflect with humor, Olivia, but the only one you're hiding from is yourself." He stepped closer, kissed me on the side of the forehead, and turned to walk away. "Have a good night. I'll see you in the morning."

I walked into the apartment and headed straight for the bathroom to wash my face and brush my teeth. I needed to go to bed and try to forget the thing I wasn't supposed to have seen.

I slipped into bed five minutes later and closed my eyes.

That was a mistake because the only thing I could see was Addison and Maddox together.

I sighed and rolled over. "Think of something else," I whispered to myself.

I closed my eyes again, and this time, I saw Tommy. He was sitting around the patio table, as he had been earlier tonight.

This was a much better thought.

Unfortunately, it didn't last. Tommy picked me up, carried me into the living room, and set me down on the same couch Addison and Maddox had been having sex on previously. He pulled off his shirt, and I flung my eyes open.

Okay, so I just needed to do something before going to bed. My adrenaline was still a little high from walking home. I had joked with Addison that morning about not having time for television, but I was on vacation. I should really find one of the shows that people had talked about around the office.

I threw back the covers and padded through the dark living room to find my laptop. I couldn't find my computer at first, and then I remembered I had left it in the kitchen. I had been on a quick conference call with my assistant as I put away my groceries.

I picked it up off the counter and turned to go back to my room, so I could watch TV in bed, but I stopped when I saw the light on in the apartment where Tommy was staying. Curious as to what he was doing, I moved closer to my window.

And gasped.

Tommy had just stripped off his shirt. Kind of like he had in my little fantasy minutes ago. But unlike my fantasy, I didn't want to make the image disappear, and I didn't step away either.

He turned, so his side was facing me, and I watched as Tommy pushed his shorts off. I gasped again. He wasn't wearing underwear.

His muscular thigh flexed as he lifted his leg to pull his shorts from his foot, and I remembered how it had felt against the palm of my hand when we were at Addison and Maddox's. It felt exactly how it looked.

Tommy spun around and faced the window. He walked toward it, and I only had a couple seconds to look before he closed the shade, but it was enough.

His dick was fucking huge.

I spun and threw my back against the wall.

Something was wrong with me. First, I had spied on Addison and Maddox and now Tommy.

I had never been a voyeur before, but it seemed like I was trying to hit a new world record.

"*You need to get laid,*" a voice that sounded an awful lot like Addison said in my head. "*You need to find a man who fucks you like Maddox fucks me.*"

I squeezed my eyes shut. My brain was playing tricks on me.

No, it isn't. It's trying to tell you something, but you're not listening.

My eyes popped open.

Could this fake Addison be right? Was I ignoring what my body was trying to tell me?

Tommy's words came back to me about lying to myself.

I slowly ran my free hand down my body and paused when I reached my pajama shorts.

Just do it.

I slid my hand underneath and put it between my legs.

I was soaked.

My body was trying to tell me that I was horny, and I had been ignoring it. Not that I was surprised. I hardly ever masturbated, even in between relationships. I was usually too busy.

But being on vacation made it harder to push sexual thoughts—sexual frustrations—away.

I pulled my hand from my shorts and contemplated what to do.

Addison had said she'd invited me here to get laid by Tommy.

I mean...could I really do that?

"Screw it." I set my laptop on the kitchen table, grabbed my phone from the nightstand, and locked the door behind me.

11

TOMMY

K *nock, knock.*

I set my book down and looked at my watch. It was way too late for visitors.

But I also wasn't worried. Intruders rarely took the time to knock.

I pulled on the shorts I'd been wearing earlier and went to my door. "Who's there?"

"Olivia." She sounded scared.

I scrambled to unlock the door and pulled it open as fast as I could. "Are you okay?" I asked before I could even see her face.

She nodded. Then shook her head. Then nodded again. She laughed. "I don't know how to answer that."

I almost lost my train of thought as I noticed her nipples poking through her satin pajama top. *Concentrate, Morelli. Something's obviously wrong.*

I stepped aside. "Come in."

She slipped past me, and I swore I could smell her sex.

And now, I was getting hard with no shirt to cover my budding erection.

I cursed silently and stuck my upper body out my door just to make sure my stairwell was clear.

Everything seemed safe, so I closed my door and locked it. I crossed my hands over my now-apparent manhood, hoping that I wasn't actually drawing attention to it. "What's wrong?"

She wrung her hands. "Nothing's wrong per se. But I think I want to answer your question."

I wasn't sure what question she was referring to. She couldn't possibly be talking about...

"*What did you mean when you said you'd never had sex like that?* That question?"

"Yes."

I raised my hands and immediately brought them back down. "Okay, it's not that I'm not curious—because I totally am—but you seem to be a little wound up. It's really none of my business, Liv. You don't have to answer it. Not if it's going to upset you."

She shook her head. "I'm not upset. I'm amped up."

"About what?"

"Just let me get this out, okay?"

I bit the inside of my cheek to keep from laughing. "Okay."

She began pacing back and forth. "I've never had sex like Addison and Maddox. It was so...hot."

I sighed. I didn't want her beating herself up because of what I'd said when I met her years ago. At least that took care of my cock standing at attention. Nothing like guilt to get that guy to go into hiding.

"Olivia, I'm sorry. I never meant to give you a complex."

She stopped pacing and stared at me. "This has nothing to do with you, Tommy."

Oh-kay. "Noted."

"This has to do with what I saw this evening. The passion between the two of them…"

I dared to lift a finger. "Can I bring up one thing?"

"What?" She looked annoyed.

"They're married. And very much in love. You can't compare your relationships to what Maddox and Addison have because not many people have that. Not even other married couples."

She narrowed her eyes at me and took a step closer. And another and another until we were almost touching. "You're not listening."

"I am, but I don't know what you're trying to tell me." *Apparently.*

She put her hands on my chest and shoved me back against the door. "Addison and Maddox had hot sex like that, even back when they hated each other."

"But they were still secretly in love—"

Her fingernails dug into my skin. Her message was received. I was shutting up.

"Please continue."

She looked me in the eye. "As I was saying, I've never had anyone fuck me like that. I've never even gotten off during sex. And I've never been spanked. I know I've never had my pussy pounded."

I didn't even know what to say to that. I had a feeling if I said I was sorry, she'd cut my balls off.

Unfortunately, my dick wasn't getting the message because I was hard again. Watching her boss me around was such a turn-on because if I ever did get her naked, I would turn things around so—

She pushed her pelvis into mine. "I want you to fuck me like that. I want you to do all the things you thought I needed the first time you met me."

I wrapped my hands around her back, flipped us around, and pushed her back against the door. "Why didn't you say so?" I ran a thumb over her lips. "I'm going to fuck you so good."

12

OLIVIA

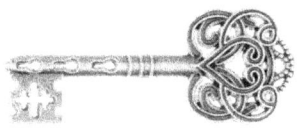

A thrill ran up my spine and through my body.

Tommy met my eyes. "First, I want you to know that I'm going to expand your boundaries and maybe push against them a little. But at any time, if I go too far, you just tell me to stop, and I will."

I nodded.

The corner of his mouth turned up. "Good girl. Agreeing with me already."

He picked me up, and I wrapped my legs around his waist. I could barely cross my ankles as he carried me to the bedroom.

"Have you ever had an orgasm?"

"What? Of course I have."

"Just checking." He kissed my neck. "Have you ever had a non-boring orgasm?"

"They're orgasms. How can they be boring?"

He chuckled. "You'd be surprised." He set me down on my feet. "Take off your clothes."

I looked around the room. He had a lamp on next to his bed. "Can we turn the light off?"

I usually had sex in the dark or with some of my clothes on. It wasn't that I was self-conscious about my body. It just felt strange to be naked with someone who could see all of me.

Tommy smiled and shook his head. "No." He made a gesture with his hand. "Strip."

I bit my lip. I was already feeling like my boundaries were being pushed, and I was glad he'd warned me. But it definitely wasn't enough for me to stop what was happening. This was what I had come here for anyway.

I slowly took off my pajamas, keeping my eyes on Tommy as he watched me strip. His eyes burned with desire when I took off my top, and he licked his bottom lip when I pushed my bottoms off.

He stepped close to me. "Olivia, do you trim?" His voice was teasing.

"Yes. Why?"

"Because I didn't expect it from you."

"I like it that way."

"Baby, you don't have to justify it to me. I like it that way, too." He brushed the hair over my cleft. "Not short, not too long, perfect." He lifted his chin. "Get on the bed. Lie down. On your back."

I crawled to the middle of the bed and did as he'd commanded. And then it was my turn to watch.

Tommy had taken his shirt off before I arrived, so I'd been admiring his muscular chest since I walked in. And with two flicks of his wrists, he was naked, too.

I'd already known his dick was big from seeing it through

my window, but that hadn't prepared me to see it in person. Not only was it long, but it was thick, too.

I totally understood his nickname now.

He was going to kill me with that thing.

"Hey, hey," Tommy said, and he knelt on the bed and cupped my calves. "I promise I will make sure you are good and ready for me."

I tore my eyes away from his massive erection to his face. "How do you know what I was thinking?"

"Not to sound cocky, but it's what almost every woman thinks. And the sheer terror on your face was another giveaway."

I frowned. "I'm not terrified. Just…anxious."

"I understand that." He spread my knees apart. "Beautiful."

I liked hearing him say that about me.

He dropped his body over mine, and I tensed up, fearing he was going to try and enter my body but only for a moment. He kept our lower halves separated as he kissed me.

Our kisses started out as pecks, but they soon deepened as Tommy nudged my lips open and slipped his tongue in my mouth.

I was never big on French kissing, but he didn't bulldoze my mouth like some guys did. He was skillful, almost as if it was an art for him, and when he pulled away, I was left wanting more.

He kissed my chest over my breastbone and then took a nipple into his mouth.

A sound escaped from the back of my throat, and I cupped his head.

My breasts fit my frame and the rest of my body, but

because I was small, so were they. Some guys I'd dated didn't pay much attention to them because of their size, but I always wished they would because they were sensitive. I swore there was a straight line from my nipples to my vagina.

Tommy looked down on me and licked his fingers. He slid his hand between our bodies and stroked it over my clit.

I arched my back as he watched me, rubbing me over and over. Keeping his hand in place, he drew my other nipple into his mouth.

He kept up the double stimulation until I was writhing and grinding my hips on his hand. Usually, I could go forever without an orgasm, but now that one was close, I wanted it badly.

I almost cried when Tommy took his hand away, but he didn't give me much time to think about it because he gripped both of my boobs in his hands and scraped the tips with his teeth.

I was so horny now that I arched my pelvis in search of his cock. But he didn't let the two meet.

He kissed his way down my abdomen and drew my legs over his shoulders.

"What…"

He lapped his tongue over my swollen nub.

"What are you…"

He sucked on it, and I forgot to finish my sentence.

I had been trying to ask him what he was doing, going down on me. It was a rarity with the men I'd gone out with, and it usually only happened after I went down on them first.

Maybe I did need someone like Tommy. If only for a night.

I was already on edge from him using his fingers on me and was feeling super sensitive. I couldn't lie still from how good his tongue felt. But even as it looked like I was trying to buck him off, he kept his mouth on my pussy. For some reason, that was the hottest thing that had happened all night. He had an excuse to move, but it was as if he liked the taste of me and didn't want to let go.

I used my willpower and commanded my body to lie still. Tommy reached for my hand and threaded our fingers together. I squeezed tight as I watched him eat me out.

It turned out, my willpower was shot, and soon, I was squirming under him. My climax was building. My breathing was shallow, and I couldn't stop the little cries from leaving my mouth.

I was getting so close that I twisted my body, and this time, Tommy sat up.

"I'm sorry," I said breathlessly. "Please don't stop."

He ran his hand down my side as he got behind me. "Don't worry. It's not over. But the wait is going to make you come that much harder."

Grabbing my hand, he brought it between my legs. I flinched. I was so swollen, and I thought my clit was going to explode. He pushed two of my fingers inside me.

"Feel how wet you are." He pressed his own finger in next to mine. "Feel how much you can take."

He didn't wait for me to follow his commands. He just took our hands and wrapped them around his cock.

He groaned. "Even your hand feels good."

I smiled. I liked knowing that I had that power over him.

He guided his thick length in between my legs, my hand still on him. He swirled the head of his shaft between my lips, and I actually felt wetness slide out of me. That had never happened to me before.

Tommy lifted my hand and kissed the back of it, and he slowly drove his cock into me.

I cried out, and he wrapped his arms around me. I thought he was afraid he'd hurt me, but it was the opposite. Nobody had ever felt that good inside me.

I took a cue from him and kissed the arm that was above my breasts, letting him know I was okay.

He got the message and started rotating his hips. "Fuck. I knew you'd feel good, but I had no idea."

I grinned in satisfaction and wasn't prepared for the slap that landed on my ass. "Holy shit."

"You can't get all smug yet. We haven't even made each other come."

"But—"

Smack.

I cursed again. There was stinging on my backside, but it didn't hurt like I would have expected it to. Maybe it was because he never stopped pumping his hips as he fucked me.

I had an *aha* moment as I realized he was giving me exactly what I had asked for.

The only thing that would make it better was if I could come while having sex.

As if he could read my thoughts, he lifted my leg back over his hip. He ran his hand over my thigh, down my body, and in between my legs. He used all four fingers to rub my clit with the same rhythm he drove into me.

Tommy kissed my shoulder and ran his teeth over my neck. "Are you going to come?"

I shook my head, even as I was grinding my hips against him.

He laughed. "I'm going to make you regret lying to me

later. But right now, I'm going to give you exactly what you need."

He stopped rubbing my swollen nub and pinched it between two fingers.

I screamed out as my whole body shattered. My arms and legs shook, and my belly quivered. Part of me thought I was dying, but then I realized it would be a wonderful way to die.

I was still shaking a little as Tommy flipped me on my back, rolled on top of me, and thrust back into me. He pushed my knees to my head and pounded into me until he exploded inside of me.

13

TOMMY

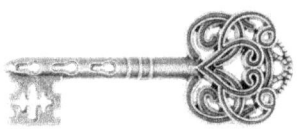

The next morning, I woke up all alone, which was surprising. Not because Olivia was gone, but because I hadn't woken up when she snuck out. Because that was the only way someone was getting by a Navy SEAL. Even a retired one.

The sun was barely up, but the store opened at six a.m., and I'd told Olivia we'd be going to Des Moines early. The only problem was that I didn't have her phone number. I sure hoped Maddox or Addison was awake to send it to me.

Then, I remembered they had kids, so of course, one of them would be awake.

I sent a group text to both, asking for Olivia's number.

Within a minute, Addison replied with the info along with a reminder.

> Addison: Remember, no more than 30 minutes at her office, or you're carrying her out of there.

> Me: Got it, boss.

Addison: Thank you for acknowledging my
superiority.

I laughed and started a new text message.

Me: Are you awake?

I pushed back the covers and sat up. Just as I realized
that I could smell Olivia's desire on me, my phone beeped.

Olivia: Who is this?

How to answer that one? I could come out and tell her
Tommy right away, or I could mess with her a little.

Me: Who do you think it is?

Olivia: I don't have time for games.

Me: Sure you do.

She had last night.

Olivia: Listen here. My friend is a sheriff with
the local county, and I am this close to
calling him and reporting your ass.

I laughed. I didn't think she'd mess with me back.

Me: You can give him my number, but he
already has it.

Olivia: Tommy?

I frowned. I'd thought she already knew it was me.

Me: Yes, Tommy. Who did you think it was?

Olivia: You.

Hmm. I didn't quite believe her, but I could be wrong. I couldn't see her face or hear her voice. Rather than push her on it, I changed the subject.

Me: When will you be ready to go?

Olivia: I'm ready now.

I should have known.

Me: I need to shower, and then I'll be over soon.

Olivia: Just text me when you're done. I'll meet you outside.

———

Fifteen minutes later, I headed downstairs, ready to walk over to Maddox and Addison's to get the vehicles. But when I walked outside, I saw that they were both there.

"Hey," Olivia said, coming over to me. She handed me the keys. "I walked over there this morning, and Addison and I drove both of the vehicles back."

I studied her. She looked a lot like the first time I'd met her. Hair up, fancy suit on, and uptight.

You would have never known that this woman had been a sweaty mess last night in bed. Or that she had screamed so loud that I was half-deaf in one ear this morning.

In fact, she was acting like nothing had happened

between us. She wasn't blushing or looking at me coyly. She was business as usual.

I had half a mind to spin her around, bend her over the hood, and lift up her skirt just to see if my handprint was still on her ass.

She snapped her fingers in front of me. "Tommy."

I shook off any thoughts of getting Olivia naked. "Yeah?"

"I said, are you okay to drive?" She patted her laptop bag. "I'm going to do a little work on the way there."

"Yes, I'm okay to drive."

As if I ever wasn't going to be the one behind the wheel. She was riding with me, not the other way around. And I didn't like that she was going to use her job to avoid talking to me.

I'd been inside her, damn it, and now, she was trying to pretend like I hadn't made her come so hard that her whole body trembled.

I snatched the keys out of her hand and thought about not unlocking it until she acknowledged that we'd had sex last night.

But she was already opening the door. Of course she had already unlocked it.

I stomped over to the driver's side and got in. "Put on your seat belt," I snapped.

She narrowed her eyes at me as she pulled the belt over her. "Jeez, someone woke up on the wrong side of the bed this morning."

Maybe because someone was rude and snuck out of it first.

I thought it but didn't say it. She would use it as an excuse to get into a fight and not talk to me. And I wasn't going to let her pretend like we hadn't fucked all night.

I kept my eyes on the road as I started Maddox's SUV

and backed out of the parking spot. "Nah. I was just up all night, handing out orgasms like they were fucking candy." I smirked as I put the vehicle in drive. "But then again, there's nothing new about that."

14

OLIVIA

I opened my laptop with a sigh. I knew that Tommy was upset, but I didn't have time to coddle him.

My assistant, Derek, had woken me up with an important text at five in the morning, concerning the case I'd won last month. I'd thought it was over until I got that message. It was a good thing we were already going to Des Moines; otherwise, I would have gone on my own.

I was keeping my promise to Addison that I would come back, but there was a strong chance I'd have to convince Tommy to let me stay longer than half an hour.

"I was thinking, why don't you drop me off at my office while you go and pick up the windows? Since you don't need my help."

He turned his head and scowled at me. "You get a half hour, remember?"

I'd had no idea men could be so touchy about sex. But I also couldn't tell if he wanted me to acknowledge how great he was in the sack or if he didn't like the fact that I'd left before he woke up.

There was *no way* I was going to tell him that he had given me the best sex of my life. Absolutely not. I was not going to feed into his ego. Men were born with spoon-fed egos just for being men, but I could explain to him why I had left so early. I did realize that men also had feelings, and I might have hurt Tommy's.

"I know that's what we agreed upon, but something has come up at work. I might need a little more time."

His jaw clenched, and I knew I was going to have to explain further to get him to understand.

"Recently, I had a case where a young man was wrongly accused of killing his girlfriend. She was sixteen, and he's seventeen. Despite everything pointing to someone else committing the crime—DNA didn't match, fingerprints didn't match, my client had an alibi—her family was —*is*— convinced that he did it. And they will not let it go even though we won and he can never be tried again because of double jeopardy."

My client, Tate Garrett, had been accused of killing his girlfriend, Annabelle Scott. Her father, Gary Scott, had a lot of pull. Tate's case reminded me a little bit of Addison. Her father was rich and hated Maddox, just like Gary and his wife, Miranda, hated Tate. Thankfully, Addison hadn't been a victim though.

I waited for Tommy to tell me no, but he asked, "If there was so much evidence against him, how did he get arrested and charged in the first place?"

"Her father's a rich white man. He's friends with the mayor and the district attorney."

"Ah. And I'm guessing your client isn't white?"

I chuckled. "No, actually, he's white, too. I can sometimes get passionate about that particular subject because I'm a woman of color." I shrugged. "No offense."

"None taken. I'm not white."

I looked him up and down and laughed. "Yes, you are."

"Actually, Miss Know-It-All, I'm part Native American and part Filipino."

"That explains the dark hair and eyes."

"Well, I'm also Italian and Greek, so there's that, too."

"Now, if only we could take care of the man part, then you'd be perfect," I joked.

He snorted. "You didn't seem to mind the man part last night when it was deep inside you, sweetheart."

A flush started in my cheeks and went down to my toes. I was embarrassed and turned on. A memory of waking up a few hours after we'd gone to sleep made its way to the forefront of my brain. He had woken me up with his rough hands and then rolled over and gently slid into me —

"So, you said the girlfriend's dad is rich and obviously has connections, but your client can't pull the same strings, I take it?"

Thank God he'd interrupted my thoughts. I didn't have time to think about sex.

"Yes. His mom and stepdad have decent jobs and a nice home, but they certainly don't have anything left over to keep paying attorney fees. And they definitely aren't friends with the mayor or anyone else political. I took his criminal case on pro bono, but now, her family is suing him. He can't afford that. Which is probably why they're suing him. Her parents are awful."

"What are you going to do?"

"I'm certainly not going to let them win." Not after everything that family had done.

"Are you going to represent him again for free?"

"Yes." I grinned like a Cheshire cat. "And then, when we win, I'm going to countersue for emotional damage and damage to his reputation." And any other charges I could come up with. "He lost a scholarship to college because of this case. The girlfriends' parents smear his name on the news every chance they get."

Tommy shook his head. "I will never understand that. With all the evidence, they have to know he's innocent. Yet they continue to go after him. Meanwhile, the real predator is still out there. Sometimes, they continue committing crimes. It makes me sick."

I'd had no idea he would be so passionate about something. "Maybe you should go into law enforcement like Maddox?"

He looked at me like I was nuts. "And live in a small town like him, too? No way. Brook Creek is fine to visit, but I'd go stir-crazy, living there. I grew up in New York. I need to be in a city of some sort."

"Where in New York?"

"Staten Island. And you? Have you always lived in Des Moines?"

"I was born in South Korea actually. My parents adopted me when I was about nine months old, so I've lived in Des Moines ever since, minus the years I lived in Iowa City for undergrad and law school."

"Have you ever thought about living anywhere else?"

I rolled it around in my brain. "Not really, no. You?"

He shrugged. "No. Right now, I'm still in Virginia, and I know I probably won't stay there. Not now that I'm retired. But I don't want to go back to New York either. I haven't decided what I'm going to do yet. All I know is that nothing will compare to being in the Navy."

I felt bad for Tommy. It was hard enough to figure out what you wanted to do for the rest of your life when you were young and idealistic. But giving up a career you loved and then trying to find a second career that you were never going to like as much would be even harder.

"I'm sorry," was all I said.

He smiled way too big. "Hey, don't feel sorry for me. I'll get it all sorted." He looked down at my computer. "Why don't you get to work? You have a client who is counting on you."

15

TOMMY

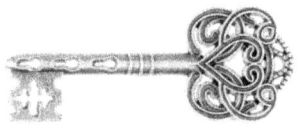

I decided to be the nice guy and dropped Olivia off at her firm before I went and picked up the windows. It didn't take me very long, so I ran a few more errands before I went back to her office. There was a little something I wanted to buy before Olivia and I got naked again.

When I arrived back at her office and went up to her floor, I had to admit, I was impressed. For some reason, I always pictured a small office—perhaps because of Addison—but Olivia had a whole firm with receptionists at the front desk, people buzzing around, and a sign up above that said *Mayer, Hastings, & Lee.*

"Can I help you?" a woman behind the desk asked.

"Oh, sorry. Name's Tommy, and I'm here for Olivia Mayer."

"Please have a seat while I call her."

Almost fifteen minutes later, a nicely dressed man came into the waiting room, and I could tell he was headed straight for me. Olivia had already left me hanging with no word from her, and it looked like she was going to pawn me off on someone else.

"Thomas Morelli?"

"Uh…" No one called me Thomas, and it sounded strange. "You can call me Tommy," I said as I stood.

I towered over the guy, but he still looked up to me and said, "Mr. Morelli it is." He spun on his heel. "Right this way."

We made our way past several offices and conference rooms until we got to the corner office.

The man knocked on the door and opened it before she could respond. "Mr. Morelli is here to see you."

I walked in as Olivia was standing behind her desk, shuffling papers around.

"Who's the suit?" I asked.

She paused long enough to look up at me. "Huh?"

I pointed behind my shoulder. "Who's the suit? The guy who brought me here."

A piece of hair had fallen over her face, and she stuck her lower lip out and blew it to the side. "Oh, that's my assistant, Derek. Didn't you meet him when we came for Maddox's case?"

"No."

"Oh. Okay." She went back to her search.

"I told him to call me Tommy, but he refused."

"Yeah, he thinks it's a ridiculous name for a grown man. I told him he could call you Tom, but I wasn't sure if you'd answer." She pulled out a stack of papers paper-clipped together. "*Yes*. I found it."

I walked further into her office. "You don't think my name is ridiculous for a grown man, do you?"

She was flipping through her pile, licking her fingers

every few pages for a better grip, yet she still managed to hear me. "Kind of. It makes me think of a kid. But I suppose I know you now, so it kind of fits who you are."

"Gee, thanks."

She stopped and looked up at me. "I'm sorry. When I'm working, I either don't hear when people talk to me or I answer really honestly."

I laughed. "Good to know. And I happen to like Tommy. Thomas is too formal, and Tom was my grandfather."

She smiled. "Tommy it is then. Like I said, it suits you."

I looked at my watch. "So, are you about ready to go? I've given you almost two hours. Addison is going to be mad."

She winced. "I'm almost done, I swear. I think I found what I needed. I'm going to have Derek and Anita start working on things while I'm gone, so I can jump right in when I get back."

"Who's Anita?" I didn't know why I'd asked. It wasn't like it mattered.

"She's one of our investigators," Derek said as he walked in behind me. "And don't listen to her. She's never 'almost done.'" He used air quotes. "She'll stay here all night if you let her."

"That's not true," Olivia said to me. She looked at Derek. "What do you have there?"

"With everything going on, I forgot to tell you that I'd picked up your mail from home yesterday. I didn't know if you wanted to look at it or for me to save it until you came back from your vacation."

"Save it," I said at the same time she said, "I'll look at it now."

"Olivia," I said.

"It'll only be a minute," she said to me, and her assistant handed her the mail and walked out.

She started flipping through it. "Junk, junk, junk, bill that is auto paid, junk, junk—oh…what's this?" She set down all her mail, minus one piece. It looked like it had fancy writing on it.

She was smiling as she cut open the envelope, but as soon as she opened the letter inside, her smile vanished. She dropped the piece of paper and stepped back until she hit the wall. And her face was pale.

I immediately marched over to her desk and picked up the letter.

"No, don't—" she started but stopped when I gave her a hard look.

No way was I going to stand there while something had obviously upset her.

DEAR MS. MAYER,

I HAVE ASKED YOU SEVERAL TIMES TO STOP HELPING TATE GARRETT, BUT YOU JUST DON'T SEEM TO LISTEN. AND NOW, HE'S FREE, YOU STUPID BITCH.

YOU JUST COULDN'T KEEP YOUR DUMB CUNT NOSE OUT OF THIS CASE. FOR THAT, YOU WILL PAY.

MAYBE NOT TODAY AND MAYBE NOT TOMORROW, BUT I WILL GET YOU WHEN YOU LEAST EXPECT IT.

There was no name at the end.

"Who sent this to you?" I asked.

She shook her head. I didn't know if it was because she didn't want to tell me or because she didn't know, and I didn't want to press her when she looked so scared.

"Derek," I yelled.

Olivia's assistant showed up in the doorway. "*Shh*. This is a place of busi—oh crap, what's wrong?" he said as he came into the room and shut the door.

I handed him the letter. "Do you know who this is from?"

Derek quickly read it and shook his head. "No, but this isn't the first time she's gotten one. It's been going on since the case started."

I looked over my shoulder at her, and she muttered the words, "Here. Always here."

"Shit, was this in the pile of mail I brought you?" Derek asked, his eyes wide.

"Yes," I answered for her.

Derek grimaced. "He's never sent anything to her home. It's always come to the office."

So, now, this piece of shit knew where Olivia lived.

"Who is he?" I demanded.

Derek shrugged. "We don't know. We don't even know if it's a *he*. We've just been assuming it's a man." He lowered his voice. "She won't say it in the exact words, but we both think it's Tate's girlfriend's father."

I walked over to Olivia and pulled her into my arms. Even with the letter, I thought she would maybe push me away, but instead, she fisted my shirt in her hands and buried her face in my chest.

I noticed that Derek looked surprised, but I quickly put it out of my mind. We had bigger things to worry about than me comforting his boss.

I rubbed my hands over her arms and back. "We need to call the police."

16

OLIVIA

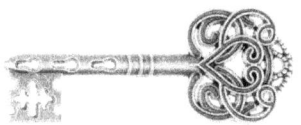

I wanted to stay in Tommy's arms and forget about the stupid letter that had been sent to my home. I wanted it to be last night—when we had been alone and in his bed, when the worst thing I'd had to worry about was how I was going to sneak out in the morning.

Not how someone had gotten my home address and sent me another threatening letter.

I should have listened to Addison and not come to the firm today.

"Olivia, did you hear me?" Tommy's chest vibrated against my ear. "We need to call the police."

I took a deep breath and stepped back. "No."

He looked at me like I had grown an extra limb. "You can't let this go. Someone sent you this." He picked up the envelope and jammed a finger at the stamp. "They mailed it. That could make it a federal case."

I snorted. "I hardly think the Feds are going to want—"

"Where are the other letters?"

R.L. KENDERSON

"I threw them away."

Fire burned in his eyes, and he looked like he wanted to kill me. "*Why*? Why would you do that? Why did you not tell the police sooner?"

I snatched the envelope out of his hand in anger. "Because that's what they want. They want me off my game. They want me worrying about my safety instead of my client's future." I stood on my tiptoes to try and get in Tommy's face even though he was a good half a foot away. "I'm not going to let that happen. I'm not going to sacrifice my client like that."

His jaw clenched. "You could have given the case to someone else."

"But that's what they want. I'm one of the best attorneys —no, *the best* attorney—and they are doing this to mess with me. And I'm not going to let them win."

Tommy raised his hands up in the air and fisted them in frustration. "Olivia, you said yourself, the case is over. Yet they're still threatening you. At home."

I shook my head. "But they're suing now. They didn't get me to quit before, so they're upping their game."

"May I interject?"

Tommy and I both turned to look at Derek. I'd forgotten he was there.

"I still have the letters," he said.

"What?" I asked.

"I…still have the letters."

"Thank God. Someone with some sense," Tommy said. "Put that letter"—he grabbed the envelope back from me— "and this envelope with the others and go call the police."

"Don't you do it, Derek," I said through clenched teeth.

"Don't listen to her. She'll thank you later."

Derek ran out of the room.

"If you call 911, I'm firing you."

Derek didn't come back.

I looked at Tommy again. I knew I'd only seen him a couple of times. Maddox's case and then Maddox and Addison's wedding, but this was the first time he looked angry.

It was a whole different side of him.

"You're making a big deal out of nothing."

"If it's not a big deal, then why did you almost pass out after reading the note?"

I narrowed my eyes. "I didn't almost pass out." It was the truth. But I also wasn't going to admit that it had scared the piss out of me. I knew that it was most likely Annabelle's father, and he wasn't actually going to hurt me, but this is the first time a letter had been delivered to my home.

Derek came back to the room. "I called the police."

Tommy breathed a sigh of relief.

"You're fired," I told him.

"No, I'm not. You said you'd fire me if I called 911. I didn't. I called a non-emergency number. Besides, you need me."

Dammit, he was right.

"You're on probation then."

He rolled his eyes at me, but I was serious. I needed to talk to him about who was his boss and who he should be taking orders from. It was just like a man to listen to another man.

"Stop looking at me like that, Olivia," Derek said. "You know it was the right thing to do."

———

Two police officers arrived about an hour later and put the letters and envelopes in an evidence bag. They took all three of our fingerprints to rule us out, but they pointed out that the sender had probably worn gloves. If we were lucky, the person had licked the envelope, but it was about a fifty-fifty shot. Then, they interviewed all three of us even though Tommy had only been around for the last one.

"Who is this guy?" Derek asked while Tommy was with the officers and we were alone.

"Hopefully, the police will find out; otherwise, this is all for nothing."

"It's not for nothing because even if there is no DNA or fingerprints, there is now a record if something happens to you. But that's not what I was asking. I meant, who is Thomas Morelli?"

"Oh." I'd been so focused on the letters that I hadn't even realized Derek was asking about Tommy.

"He's friends with Maddox and Addison Wolfe. He was one of the SEALs who helped Maddox protect that lady and her child from her ex-husband."

"I remember that. But what is he doing here, and why is he so protective of you?"

I frowned. "He's here because he had to come into town to pick up something for a project he's doing with Maddox. I hitched a ride with him. And I don't think he's so protective of *me*. He's protective in general. He's former military."

"Uh…"

I narrowed my eyes. His response made it sound like he understood, but the skepticism in his eyes said he didn't believe me.

Speaking of not believing me…

"About your probation."

He raised his eyebrows. "You can't be serious."

"I am serious. I'm your boss. What are you doing, listening to a guy you just met over me? Where's the loyalty?"

He put his hand over mine. "Olivia, I've been with you since the beginning. I left our old firm when you started this one despite not knowing when I was going to get a paycheck. You will never find someone more loyal to you than me." He held up a finger with his opposite hand. "But just because I'm loyal doesn't mean I'm going to ignore my gut instinct when it comes to your security. Because loyalty means keeping you safe, too. I've wanted to call the police since the second letter—the second out of twenty-two, I might add. Hearing another person confirm that I wasn't overreacting is what made me call." He squeezed my fingers. "Understand?"

"I suppose."

He pulled his arm away. "Now, let's put this whole probation thing behind us because you'd be lost without me."

"I'll consider it."

He laughed as the door to my office opened.

"I think we have everything we need, Ms. Mayer," one of the officers said when the three men stepped out into the hall. "Until then, do you have a security system? Somewhere you can stay?" The officer glanced at Tommy when he asked the last question.

"I'm actually staying with a friend in Brook Creek for about a week."

The officer nodded. "Good idea." He handed me a business card. "If anything comes up before I call you, please feel free to give me a ring."

I read the card. "Will do, Officer Klein. Thank you for coming."

Both officers shook all our hands and went on their way.

17

TOMMY

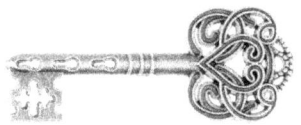

"I think we should go to your place and pick up extra clothes for you. You might end up staying in Brook Creek longer than you originally planned."

Olivia opened her mouth and looked like she was going to say no. "I'll think about it."

She wasn't happy with me right now, so I wasn't going to push. I'd work on convincing her before we left Des Moines.

I looked at my watch. It was well past lunch and heading toward dinner. "Why don't we get something to eat? I'm starving. We can worry about clothes and driving back to Brook Creek after our stomachs are full."

Olivia rubbed her head.

"Unless you need to do more work?"

"No." She dropped her hand. "It's fine. I'm just worried about Addison and Maddox. Doesn't he want his windows?"

"I already texted Maddox and told him we were going to be late and that we'd explain everything later when we got back."

Her shoulders sagged in relief. "Thank you." She looked

at her assistant. "Derek, go ahead and take the rest of the afternoon off."

"Thanks, *boss*," he said, his tone slightly mocking.

"What was that about?" I asked after Derek was gone.

"Oh, we just had a conversation about him going against my wishes while you were talking to the officer."

"Everything okay?"

She smiled softly. "With Derek? Yeah, we're good."

"So, where should we eat?"

"I'm going to need something a lot stronger than food," she answered.

———

Olivia's office was in downtown Des Moines, and when we left, we walked a few blocks to a tiny bar.

"Wow," I said, holding the door open for her.

"Don't worry; they have food. It's bar food, but it's good."

"No. I wasn't saying that because I'm hungry, although that is good to know. I was saying that because it doesn't look like your kind of place."

It was clean but very dark and old. Classic rock filled the room. I took Olivia for more of a classical-music kind of woman.

It was a Thursday, late afternoon, but there were more people in the bar than I'd thought there would be. It wasn't crowded though, and we found two free stools at the end of the bar, near the wall.

There was a stack of menus on the bar top, and Olivia grabbed two and handed one to me.

"Maybe you don't know me as well as you think you do," she said to me. Thankfully, the music playing wasn't too loud, so neither of us had to yell to hear each other. "We might have met a few years ago, but we haven't spent that much time together."

"Maybe I'll just have to get to know you better."

She flipped over her menu. "We'll see about that."

I looked at my own menu. "Why do you say that?"

She put her elbow on the bar and her chin in her hand. "A couple reasons."

At that moment, a bartender came over and asked us what we wanted.

"I'll take an old-fashioned."

I raised my eyebrows.

"What?"

"I saw you as more of a wine drinker."

"I like wine. It's just not all I like."

The bartender slid her drink over. "And for you, sir?"

"I'll have a whiskey, neat."

"I saw you as more of a beer drinker," Olivia said to me.

"Touché." I leaned close to her ear and said, "I like beer. It's just not all I like."

"Here is your drink, sir. Do either of you want to order food?"

We requested several appetizers because I was a big boy and needed lots of calories to keep me fueled.

"I'll put your order in," the bartender said. "It'll be about fifteen to twenty minutes."

"Thank you," Olivia said.

After the bartender walked away, I asked, "What are your reasons for me not getting to know you better?"

"You don't beat around the bush, do you?"

"I think you already know that about me."

"True." She turned in her stool toward me. Whoever had

bought them went the cheap route because they didn't swivel. She rested her arm on the back of the chair since it was now at her side. "My first reason is that you were a little high-handed back at my office. I said I didn't want to call the police, and you didn't listen to me. You didn't respect my wishes. And the second reason is, you said you were going to test my boundaries last night. While I admit that the sex was good, I had expected a little more."

I tilted my head and studied her. "Noted." I shifted in my seat to face her, too. "I'm sorry that I didn't respect your wishes, but when it comes to someone's life, I'm never going to ignore a threat. Not even if it were Maddox or someone else from my old team. Understand?"

She nodded. "Yes. I figured you'd say as much. Derek said something similar."

I laughed. "Of course, you scolded him for not listening to you, too."

She lifted a shoulder. "I am the one in charge."

"As for your second issue"—I pulled her stool over to mine until her chair hit my knees—"who said I was going to push all your boundaries in one night?"

Her breathing deepened as her mouth opened slightly. "No one. I just assumed…"

"Uh-uh-uh. Hasn't anyone ever told you not to assume anything?" My leg was on the outside, and I moved it up a rung to block anyone from seeing what I was about to do. I ran my hand up her thigh that was facing the bar, and I put that leg over my inside knee and spread my legs to open hers.

"What are you going to do?"

I didn't answer. Rather, I continued moving up her leg, switching from the outside to the inside and up her skirt.

When I reached her underwear, I hooked my fingers in it and ripped the material apart.

Her eyes grew wide.

"Sorry. I don't like anything in the way of my workspace."

"Wh—"

I pushed two fingers inside her.

"Holy shit," she said as she bucked against my hand.

I leaned close. "Be careful. People are watching," I teased.

"Then, stop touching me."

"Not a chance." I curved my fingers toward, and within two seconds, I found the spongy spot inside her that was her G-spot.

"Oh God." Her head fell back.

"Olivia." I snapped my fingers.

She looked up, and I looked at my watch.

"The food will be here in ten minutes. If you don't come by then, you're going to have to suffer the whole ride back to Brook Creek."

She whimpered.

"Don't worry. I have faith in you."

I rubbed her G-spot, keeping my eyes on her as she grew wetter and wetter, her special spot swelling under my fingers. She gripped the back of the chair and the bar until her knuckles were white.

It seemed like she wanted to move her hips, but I was sure she didn't dare since she was in public. I was honestly surprised she was letting me touch her. I'd thought she would push me away, but maybe she really did want me to show her a thing or two about sex.

We were inching toward the ten-minute mark, and while

I had threatened her with the female version of blue balls, I would never leave her in pain like that.

When I felt like she was as close as she was going to get to an orgasm, I slammed my thumb down on her clit, and she went off like a rocket.

She fell forward into my arms and cried out into my chest.

The angle was difficult, but I kept my hand on her, making sure I saw her climax through.

"I have your food," a young woman said from behind the bar in front of us.

I smiled. "You can just set it down."

The woman frowned. "Is she okay?"

"Yeah. She just had a rough day at work." I rubbed Olivia's back like she had been crying. "You okay to sit up now?" I asked her.

18

OLIVIA

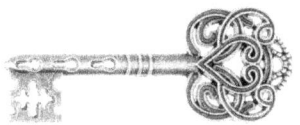

I nodded against Tommy's chest.

It was a good thing he'd told the woman who had brought our food that I had been crying because I had no idea what my face looked like.

When I sat up, Tommy pulled his fingers from my body, and I flinched at the sudden withdrawal.

I straightened my bunched-up skirt and faced forward as he did the same.

"Do you need another drink?" the woman asked.

Tommy stuck the two digits that had just been inside me into his whiskey and swirled it around. He lifted the glass and took a sip. "Nope. This is perfect."

"And you, ma'am?"

I stared at him. Even though he had just given me a fantastic orgasm, I thought watching him mix my juices with his drink was the hottest thing I'd ever seen.

"Olivia?" he said.

"Hmm?"

"The nice lady asked if you needed another drink."

"A water—" My voice was hoarse, so I cleared my throat. "A water would be great."

She smiled sympathetically at me. "Of course." She filled up a glass and pushed it in front of me. "I hope your day goes better from here on out."

I smiled. "Thank you."

Tommy was already eating but managed a muffled, "Thank you," as well.

The woman walked away, and I shifted in my seat. "I think I'd better go to the restroom and fix my makeup and hair."

Tommy reached over and ran a finger under my eye. "There. You look beautiful." He went back to his food and pushed one of the baskets I'd ordered over to me.

"How can you eat right now?" I asked in disbelief.

He wrinkled his forehead. "What do you mean?"

I leaned over to him. "After what you just did to me?"

"Got you off?" he said kind of loudly.

"*Shh.*" I scanned the room, but no one was looking at us. "Yes, that."

He smiled. "Eat, Olivia. You're going to need your strength for later."

————

I nibbled on my food at first, but soon, I discovered that I was famished. Tommy and I finished our drinks and all our food in comfortable silence.

I was actually done before he was, and for it being still early in the night, I was getting tired.

"You ready to head back to Brook Creek?"

I'd been thinking about that while we were eating. "Can I tell you something that is going to sound a little weird?"

"Always."

"Even after getting that letter today, I really want to go and stay at my house tonight." I lifted a shoulder. "I don't know. It's as though I don't like the fact that someone can scare me out of my own home, you know?"

Tommy didn't say anything, and I looked down at my hands, embarrassed.

"I know; it's stupid. Let's pay the bill, and we'll get on the road." I summoned my courage and lifted my head. "I do need to go back to the office to grab my computer and briefcase."

He lifted his hand for the bartender to come over. "I parked by your building, so we need to head back that way anyway."

"Thanks."

He put his hand on my knee. "And if you really want to stay at your place tonight, we can."

A slow smile spread across my face. "We can?"

He rolled his eyes. I felt like it was more at himself than me. "Why not?" He looked at me. "But I'm sleeping in the same bed with you to make sure you're safe. No sneaking out."

I tried not to smile. I liked the idea of him sleeping in my bed.

A stern look crossed over his face. "Please tell me you have a security system."

I shook my head.

He sighed. "*Olivia*. Even without the threats you've been getting, your job—"

I started laughing. "Fooled ya."

"That's not funny. I don't want to have to constantly worry about you when I go back to Virginia."

My first thought was, I didn't want him to go back to Virginia.

My second thought was that my first thought was silly. He had to go back to Virginia. He lived there.

The bartender brought our bill, and Tommy and I fought over who was going to pay.

"I'm the reason you're here, eating," I argued.

"But I ordered more food than you."

"How about we split it?"

He sighed, probably realizing he wasn't going to win. "Fine." He put some money down on the bar. "We need to go to a store, so I can get some things before we go to your house."

"Kinky things?" The question popped out before I could stop it.

He chuckled. "I was thinking more like a toothbrush."

"Oh."

He put his arm around me and led me out. "Don't be so disappointed. I already did my kinky shopping this morning."

I laughed. "That's funny."

"That's what you think."

I looked at him in confusion, but he didn't say anything more.

19

TOMMY

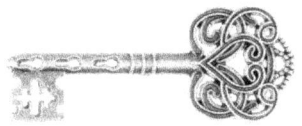

Olivia and I were in the health section at Walmart, picking up a toothbrush and a few other toiletries for me.

"I also need to go back to the books."

"What for?"

"Since I didn't know we were staying here tonight, I left my book at home. I need something else to read." I grabbed a deodorant, dropped it in my basket, and took off for the back of the store.

"Why don't you read on your phone? They have apps for that, you know."

"That's blasphemy."

She laughed. "For suggesting you read on your phone?"

"Yes. I would never do that to my books."

"You're a strange man."

"Why?"

She shook her head and smiled. "Because I can't believe that—"

I stopped walking and faced her. "That I'd be a reader?"

I finished her sentence. "Yeah, a lot of people think I'm a big, dumb jock because of the way I look. I'll have you know, I was salutatorian of my class." I took off, walking faster now.

Sometimes, people assuming I was unintelligent worked in my favor. But I didn't like it coming from Olivia.

She ran to catch up to me. "Tommy."

I kept moving.

She put her hand on my arm. "Tommy, stop."

I halted and looked at her. "What?"

"I don't think you're stupid."

I narrowed my eyes at her.

"I'm serious. I thought some bad things about you, but that's not one of them."

"Then, what were you going to say?"

"If you had let me finish, I was going to say, I can't believe people read physical books anymore."

"Oh." I had overreacted. "Sorry."

"It's okay. I'm guessing, that's happened to you before? Where someone assumes you lack intelligence?"

"Once or twice."

"I'm sorry people do that. I have the opposite problem. Everyone thinks I'm super smart because I'm Asian."

I wrinkled my forehead. "But you are smart."

She leaned forward and whispered, "But I'm horrible at math. There's a reason I became an attorney and not a doctor or scientist."

I chuckled. "Come on. Let's go look at the books."

We made our way to the books and started looking around.

"We can always go to Barnes & Noble if you can't find what you want here."

I picked up a book and started reading the synopsis. "Nah, I'm okay. I'll find something. Thanks for the offer."

I looked at about six books before I decided on two. One was the book I had been reading since the plane ride here—I didn't care about spending money on another copy—and the second book was for when I finished my current read.

"I'm ready," I said. "Do you need anything else before we leave?"

"Nope. I'm good."

We left the book aisle, but I stopped in my tracks when I saw who was standing over by the video games.

Hasn't enough bad stuff happened today?

"What's wrong?" Olivia asked me.

I pointed in the opposite direction of where we wanted to go. "Let's go that way. I'll explain later."

"Ok—"

"Hey, asshole."

"Fuck," I said under my breath. "Hold this." I handed her my shopping basket.

I stepped around her and squared my shoulders. "Frank."

The asshole from the airport just had to be here at the same time I was. At least he was alone.

"Lucky meeting you here."

"I would more go with unlucky."

Frank barked out a laugh. "You're funny. Which is good because you need to make up for the fact that you're a pussy." Frank looked around me, trying to see Olivia.

I tried to block her, but she made it easy on him by stepping out beside me.

"Your man is a pussy, did you know that?" Frank grinned. "Did he tell you about what happened at the airport and how I almost kicked his ass?"

I knew I shouldn't say anything because someone like this was just looking for trouble, but my pride wouldn't let it slide. "For fuck's sake. You didn't almost kick my ass. I told you I didn't want to fight."

And when I thought the situation couldn't be worse, Franny showed up. "What's this dickhead doing here?"

"He's trying to tell me I didn't almost kick his ass last week," he told his sister.

She snorted. "He's lying. Like when he said he didn't touch me."

"How do you two function when you are constantly getting your facts wrong?"

"What do you mean?" Frank asked.

The fact that he was asking me instead of telling me I didn't know what I was talking about proved that I was right.

"First of all, I never said I didn't touch you," I said to Franny.

I saw Olivia's head jerk back at my words and tried not to wince. *Let me finish explaining, Liv.*

Franny snickered. "Ha."

I sighed. "I said, I technically touched you, Franny, because you'd tried to touch me first. On my dick. I simply removed your hand from my private area. So, yes, I touched you but not in the way you are implying. You were the perpetrator, not me."

Franny's face turned red, and she clenched her fists.

"And, Frank, I'm not a pussy." I pointed to my chest. "See, I am smart enough to know when to fight and when not to fight. I was literally trained to do these things. And you, Frank, are not worth fighting." I grabbed Olivia's hand. "Let's go. I'm done with these two."

As we walked away, I heard Franny say, "Are you just going to let him talk to you like that?"

"Shut up, whore."

Olivia stopped and tried to pull her hand out of mine.

"Liv, they are not worth it."

"But he just called his girlfriend a whore."

"Actually, she's his sister."

Olivia's mouth fell open. "That doesn't make it any better."

"I know. It's awful, and he's a dick, but there's no point in arguing with them."

"You're right."

I took a breath in relief. "Thank you."

I moved to keep walking, but Olivia yanked on my hand again.

This time, she succeeded in getting her hand away from mine.

"Shit," I said as I followed her back to Frank and Franny.

"You, sir, are the pussy. Only a pussy would call a woman a whore, especially his sister."

"Shut up, bitch."

Olivia gasped.

I could see this was going to escalate quickly if I didn't do something to stop it, so I took the basket from her hand and picked her up in a fireman's hold.

"Tommy, put me down."

It was the smart thing to do because it stopped Olivia from fighting with Frank and Franny. And those two were too stunned to do anything more than stand there and stare at us.

"I told you, they're not worth it."

"He can't go around, calling women whores and bitches."

"I understand, but this is a fight you're never going to win."

She was silent.

But I didn't trust it.

"You can put me down."

"Nope. I don't believe you. Last time you agreed with me, you marched back there and yelled at Frank."

"You can't just carry me through the store."

"I already am. Besides, Addison gave me permission."

"It was a joke."

"Oh no, she was serious."

"If anyone looks up my skirt and sees my ripped underwear and vagina, I'm going to kill you."

"Don't worry. Your skirt is long enough to cover you. No one gets to see that pretty pussy but me."

"Tommy, you can't say stuff like that in public."

We were at the front of the store now, and a couple of heads turned our way.

"Shh…everyone's looking at you," I said as we reached the cash registers. I opted for the self-checkout.

"They're looking at you because you're carrying me."

"Ma'am, are you okay?" a lady behind me asked. "Do I need to call security?"

"It's tempting," Olivia said. "But I'm fine. He just has a protective streak."

I quickly ran my things over the scanner and paid for my stuff while Olivia assured the lady that she was safe. I was a little worried someone would stop me at the door and accuse me of kidnapping, but the greeter at the door was an older gentleman who smiled at me.

"I was married once," he told me.

"We're not married," Olivia corrected the man.

The gentleman laughed. "Don't let her go," he said to my back. "She's a keeper."

"Sexist pig," she muttered once we were outside.

"He just said you were marriage material. That's a compliment." I carried Olivia to the SUV and set her down, but I caged her in with my body. "Are you going to run back in there?"

She crossed her arms over her chest. "And give you the satisfaction of carrying me out again? No way."

"Good." I rotated my shoulder. "Because you're heavy," I teased.

She socked me in the gut. "Just get in and drive."

20

OLIVIA

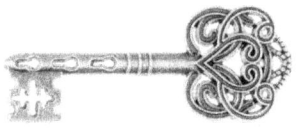

J was still fuming as Tommy drove to my house. I really, really hated being called a bitch.

I knew that Frank guy didn't know me and had just called me a bitch because I had confronted him, but that word and I went way back.

I'd been called a bitch a lot in my life. Women had called me that because I didn't want to hang out with them in high school. And guys had called me that because I didn't want to go out with them. Just because I'd had better things to do with my time than party every weekend didn't mean I was a bitch. And I shouldn't let it bother me anymore. When I was a bitch, it was usually in court, and it helped me win a lot of the time. But my teenage self still hadn't come to terms with the insult.

"You okay over there?" Tommy asked.

"I'll be fine. I just hate assholes, is all."

He put his hand on my thigh. "Me, too."

It was at this time that I realized I wasn't the only one who had been called names. "You okay?"

He looked at the rearview mirror and then at me. "Yeah. Why wouldn't I be?"

"Because of those assholes."

"Oh." He laughed as he looked in the mirror again. "Nah, I've dealt with way worse people than them. They're not worth our time and energy."

I watched him look in the mirror one more time. "Why do you keep looking in the mirror?"

"Just making sure that no one is following us."

I gasped and turned around. "Do you really think Frank and Franny are following us?"

"No. I'm afraid whoever sent you those letters is following you."

A chill went up my spine. For a few hours, I had put the threats out of my head.

Tommy squeezed my thigh. "Don't worry. No one is behind us."

I was grateful that he was trying to comfort me, but I still couldn't stop the images in my mind of someone following me home and breaking into my house. But then again, they didn't have to follow me. They already knew where I lived.

And now, I had to wonder if I had led them there.

Have I been trailed without knowing?

I liked to think I was aware of my surroundings, but sometimes, my mind was caught up in my work, and I didn't always pay close attention to the world around me.

I sighed and lay back against the headrest.

I wanted to think I was tough and didn't need help or protection, but knowing that the person sending me threatening letters knew where I lived scared the bejesus out of me. I knew that me arguing with Tommy about calling the police was just a deflection of my fright. I had really wanted to believe that it was all a ploy for Tate to lose his case and end up in prison.

I was so lost in thought that I didn't even realize we had pulled up to my house. It was a good thing I'd given him the address and he had a GPS in his phone.

Tommy went to turn off the ignition, and I put my hand on his arm.

"I'll go in and open the garage door, so you can park in the garage. If someone really knows where I live, I don't want them doing anything to Maddox's SUV."

He turned off the ignition anyway. "You're not walking into that house alone. I'll come back out and move it after I know the area is clear."

I didn't even pretend to argue because I didn't want to go in by myself either.

Tommy grabbed his bag of things he'd bought from the store, and we walked up to the front door. Everything looked the same from the outside, which was only slightly reassuring. I unlocked the door, and we stepped into my foyer, where I gave him my security code.

Tommy locked the dead bolt once we were inside. "Stay here. I'm going to check all the rooms."

I nodded.

It felt like forever for Tommy to go through my house, which wasn't even that big. When he went down into the basement, I began to wring my hands. Every horror movie I'd ever seen flashed in my brain. There could be someone hiding down there.

When I heard his heavy footsteps pounding on the stairs as he came back up, I released the breath I hadn't even realized I'd been holding.

He walked over to me and folded his big hands around my neck in comfort. "Hey, you okay?"

"I don't know."

"I know you said you wanted to stay here, but we can always go back to Brook Creek. If we do stay though, I will make sure that you are safe. This is your home, and no one should scare you out of your own place."

I let my purse slide off my shoulder and onto the floor. I wrapped my arms around his neck. "I know we don't know each other that well, but I really need you right now."

Tommy leaned down and pressed his lips against mine. "I understand." He put his arms behind my back and under my knees, picked me up, and carried me to my bedroom.

He gently laid me on my mattress and stepped back. He took off his shirt and went for his pants. I followed his lead and removed my clothes. When I got to my torn underwear, I threw them toward my bathroom. They were garbage now.

Tommy dropped down on the bed over me and took my mouth. He gently pressed his tongue against mine, and I moaned.

We kissed for a few minutes, my desire for him rising. My breasts felt heavy, and I was wet. He ran a hand down my body, thumbing my nipple and pinching it. He continued further south and grabbed his cock in his hand. He rubbed the head of his thickness against me and gently pushed inside me.

I yanked my mouth from his and threw my head back with a gasp.

He was so large, and my walls stretched to accommodate him. A few days ago, I had been afraid he would break me in two, and now, here I was, loving the way he filled me. I thought if he were even a centimeter bigger, I wouldn't be able to handle all of him, but instead, he was perfect.

I clutched at his back as he slowly thrust into me and kissed and sucked on my neck. It felt incredible to be surrounded by him, and it pushed all the bad thoughts out of my mind, just like I'd wanted it to.

I ran my hands all over Tommy's body as he began to move faster and harder. I lifted my legs, so he could drive into me deeper.

I felt and heard his breathing quicken, and I knew he was close. I wasn't going to come, but it still felt good, and I loved that my body was making him feel good, too.

When he grabbed on to my shoulders as his body shuddered and his cock jerked inside me, I held him.

We lay for about five minutes or so, just embracing each other, our bodies still connected.

Tommy stirred and gradually withdrew from my body. He kissed each of my breasts and moved off my bed to the floor. He pulled me around, so I was open to him, and without warning, he licked my pussy and sucked on my clit.

My back arched at the sudden stimulation. I was already worked up from having sex, and this was the cherry on top of the sundae.

He continued to eat me out for the next fifteen minutes or so, and I thought it was the best head of my life. The fact that he had come inside me minutes before and that he hadn't made me clean up or anything was so hot that I could climax from that thought alone.

A guy who was confident, who didn't care if his cum was on me and inside me and didn't hold back as he ate me like I was his favorite meal, was incredibly sexy.

I wanted it to last forever, but all good things had to end, so when I knew I couldn't hold off on coming any longer, I let go.

My orgasm washed over me like a wave. I pictured the way an atomic bomb started in the center and fanned out over the land. My chest was heaving, and I was so sensitive that I had to gently nudge Tommy to stop.

He stood over me, hard again, and I brushed my fingers over his erection.

He picked me up and moved me to the center of the bed before he climbed over me. I opened my legs and welcomed him into my body once more.

21

TOMMY

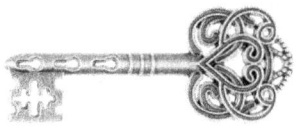

After Olivia fell asleep, I put on my jeans and moved Maddox's SUV into the garage. Then, I went around the house again to make sure every door and window was secured. Lastly, I double-checked that the security system was armed. It would be helpful if she had surveillance along with the alarm. Maybe that was something I could convince her to do in the future.

I was glad that we were going back to Brook Creek tomorrow because while Olivia might be right about her theory of who was behind her threats, I'd feel safer with her out of town.

Tomorrow was Friday, and then the weekend was Brook Days. I hoped that the fun and games would relax her some. And then, if we were lucky, the police would figure out something before she was due to return to work.

I went to the kitchen in search of something that I could make for dinner. We'd had a late lunch, but I was already hungry. Appetizers didn't fill me up for very long.

I found some beef in the freezer and noodles and

spaghetti sauce in the pantry. After a few more cupboard searches, I found the frying pan and a pot to boil water. My last find was pure luck, seeing as she might not have bread in the house when she'd planned to be gone for a week, but there was a loaf of French bread in the freezer, too.

I got to cooking and turned on the news to keep me company.

When I was finished, I went to check on Olivia. She was still sound asleep. I thought about waking her to eat but opted to keep her food warm instead. I grabbed my book out of my Walmart bag and sat down at the kitchen island to eat and read.

————

About forty-five minutes later, Olivia shuffled out of her room in my T-shirt with tired eyes.

I set my book on my chest from my spot on the recliner. "You okay?"

She ran her fingers through her hair. "Yeah. How long did I sleep?"

"I'm not sure exactly but around an hour and a half."

"Wow." She sniffed the air. "What's that delicious smell?"

"Dinner." I pointed to the kitchen. "You hungry?"

"Famished."

I grabbed my book to set it on the coffee table.

"No, please sit. I can get my own food."

"There's also garlic bread in the oven," I told her as she took a plate from the cupboard.

She turned and smiled at me. "Thank you."

I went back to reading while Olivia dished up. She went and took a seat at the stool I'd been sitting on earlier and ate in silence. I had to smile at how domesticated we seemed after hanging out for only such a short time.

About the time she was done with her food, I was at the climax of my book. I told myself just a few more pages, and then I'd go and help her clean up. But before I knew it, I turned that last page, and it was over.

"*No*," I practically whined.

"What's wrong?" Olivia said, walking over to me.

"I didn't realize the book was a series. Now, I need to go and buy the next one."

She came around my chair and sat on my lap. "You could always cave and read it as an e-book," she said with a smile.

"You're determined to convert me, huh?"

"Yes. Then, stuff like this doesn't have to happen. You don't have to wait to go to the store or to have it come in the mail. You just go on your device, and *bloop*, you have the next book."

I ran my hand up her thigh until I cupped her butt. "Bloop, huh?" I said, giving her ass a squeeze.

"Yes, bloop."

I kissed her neck and sucked on the tender skin there. "God, you smell incredible."

She sighed. "If you're trying to turn me on, it's working."

"Good." I nipped at her jaw and turned her face, so I could kiss her.

She put her hand on my chest and pushed me away. "But no sex unless you try to read an e-book."

I burst out laughing. "Are you serious?"

She tried to keep a straight face, but she smiled. "Yes. I want to introduce you to the whole new world of e-books."

I shifted her around, so she was straddling me, and I rubbed my dick against her cleft. "But I want to show you a whole new world. It's called Tommyland. There's only one ride, but it's fucking awesome."

She chuckled and put her hands on my shoulders. Then, she surprised me by grinding down on my erection.

I was ready to rip open my jeans and shove my cock inside her.

"Woman, you are killing me."

She smiled coyly. "Does that mean you'll give an e-book a try?" She bit her lower lip and slowly pulled it between her teeth.

"I transformed you into a monster." I grabbed my phone and shoved it at her. "Fine. Do what you need to do."

She made a noise of excitement and jerked the phone from my hand. "Since you're being such a good sport about this, I'll let you try my account before you decide if you want to get your own. I have a subscription service you can use to borrow some books. It might save you money."

"Good sport? You all but blackmailed me."

She just laughed as she pushed buttons on my phone. "Okay, what book are you looking for?"

I gave her the name.

"Oh shoot. It's not free." She shrugged a shoulder. "Oh well," she said and pushed a button.

I snatched my phone from her hands. "Did you just buy that for me?"

"Yes."

I watched the screen as it showed my book being down-loaded. "You didn't have to do that."

"I know. But now, you have no excuse not to read it."

I couldn't deny that I was a little excited to give it a try. But only because I could start right away and wouldn't have to wait to find a copy.

I scrolled through her library, and my mouth dropped open.

"What's wrong?"

I looked up at her. "Olivia."

She looked worried. "What? Did it not work?"

"Oh, it worked fine all right. I'm just wondering, what is this book doing on here?"

Her brow furrowed. "Which one?"

I cleared my throat like I was about to make an important announcement. I guessed I kind of was.

"*Spanked by the SEAL.*" I scrolled a little more. "*Tied Up by the SEAL.*" I gasped. "*Dominated by the SEAL*? All by someone who calls herself Scarlett Letter. Why, Olivia, you naughty girl, you." I put my phone down and looked at her with what had to be the biggest shit-eating grin on my face.

She had kinky books about Navy SEALs, and I couldn't help but feel cocky.

Her eyes were huge, her mouth was wide, and her face was the color of the spaghetti we'd had for dinner. "I downloaded them a long time ago. I haven't even read them," she adamantly denied.

Her comment didn't have the effect she'd thought it would. If the books were old, that meant she'd maybe downloaded them around the time she met me. As for not reading them…

"Well then, let's start, why don't we?"

"No."

It was too late. I was already opening up *Spanked by the SEAL*. "*As a librarian, my life was very boring,*" I began to read. "*Except for Fridays. Fridays were when Navy SEAL Flynn Bass*—Flynn Bass? What kind of name is that?" I shook my head and continued, "*Flynn Bass came in to drop off books and pick out new ones. If the library was slow, I would stare at him and fantasize about him taking me into the stacks and fucking me.*" I whistled. "Damn, this girl is a dirty librarian. Too bad she's not a dirty lawyer."

Olivia covered her face with her hands and moaned with embarrassment.

"Let's get to the good stuff." I flipped through some pages. "Ah, here we go. *Flynn ripped my dress right down the middle, and my breasts popped free, spilling right into his waiting mouth.*"

Olivia pushed off my lap. "That's it. I'm going back to bed."

"But it's just getting good."

She continued walking, so I got up and chased after her. "*Flynn shoved his face between my tits, and his pulsating cock —*"

Olivia yanked my phone out of my hand. "*Fine*. You win. No e-books." She spun and marched toward her room.

"No, wait. I want to keep reading."

"No."

I ran up behind her and picked her up.

She screamed and laughed as I tried to wrestle my phone back.

I kissed her neck for a few minutes, and her body slowly started melting into mine.

"Okay, I'll give it back." She relented. "But no more reading that book."

"What book?" I wanted to hear her say it.

"You know what book."

"Say it out loud. I'm not sure."

She sighed. "*Spanked by the SEAL.*" She shoved away from me. "You're such a butt. Making fun of a woman for what she reads."

"I thought you said you haven't read it," I teased.

"You know what I mean."

I pulled her into my arms and kissed the top of her head. "I'm sorry. You're right. You can read whatever you want. How about I make it up to you?"

She put her chin on my chest. "Oh, yeah? How are you going to do that?"

"By having *you* get spanked by a SEAL."

22

OLIVIA

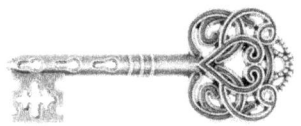

*T*he sign reading *Brook Creek — 10 miles* loomed in the distance as Tommy and I headed back. If I was being honest, I wasn't looking forward to getting a lecture from Addison about receiving threatening letters and not telling anyone.

She had already texted me several times, wanting to know more information. Apparently, Tommy had given Maddox a brief explanation of what had happened yesterday.

I knew she meant well, but I didn't want to think about those notes right now. I wanted to enjoy the rest of my little vacation. Especially since it was Friday and it was Brook Days this weekend.

"Are we going over to Addison and Maddox's right away?" I asked.

"I thought I'd stop off at my place first, so I can drop off my stuff. That okay with you?"

I sighed. "Yes. I'm not ready for Addison to give me a

speech about the letters and how I shouldn't have kept them a secret."

"Can you tell her not to?"

I shrugged. "I could, but I know she's going to do it because she's worried about me. If the situation were reversed, I'd be upset, too. I realize now that I did the wrong thing for the right reasons. No one needs to remind me that I made a mistake because I already know I did."

"Hmm," was all Tommy said.

He'd been serious this morning with packing up and making sure my house was secure before we left. He was nothing like the guy who'd teased me last night about my erotica collection. I had completely forgotten I had downloaded those books. It had been a couple of years earlier. I was very thankful that he hadn't asked me why I had downloaded them. But he'd probably already figured out it was because of him.

Even though I had been pissed about what he'd said to me the first time I met him, he had piqued a curiosity in me that I only felt comfortable exploring through literature.

I glanced at him.

At least, until recently.

We made it back to our temporary apartments, and we went our separate ways. I dropped off my laptop and the few things I'd grabbed from home.

Before I went back outside, I looked through the window into Tommy's place. It seemed like months ago that I had watched him undress instead of only a few nights.

A lot had happened in the last two days.

When I walked out the door, he was waiting for me, leaning against Maddox's SUV, typing on his phone.

"Hey," I said.

He looked up and smiled. "Hey." He stood. "You ready?"

"Yep."

When we got to Addison and Maddox's home, Tommy pulled into the driveway. After getting out, I immediately noticed the loud music coming from the house.

"What the heck?" I asked. "It's only ten in the morning."

"I guess we'll find out."

We walked into the garage, where Tommy knocked once and opened the door.

I put my hand on his arm. "What if they're having sex again?"

He laughed. "Then, I'll cover your eyes."

"I'm serious."

"Relax. They're not. I just talked to Maddox."

"If you say so."

He might be right, but I still waited for him to go inside first.

The sight that greeted us was definitely different than the last time I'd walked in. Addison and Spencer were dancing in the living room, which explained why the music was blasting from the speakers.

They didn't see us, so Tommy and I stood there, watching them for a few seconds. The two of them were pretty cute together, and I felt a tiny pang of longing for a child. That was unusual for me, as I had never been big on having kids.

Maddox came down the hall with Thane in his arms. "Hey, guys."

Addison's head whipped up. She ran over to her phone and turned off the music, and then she surprised me by rushing over and throwing her arms around me. "I'm so glad you're okay."

I hugged her back. "I'm fine."

She stepped back. "You scared me."

"I'm sorry."

She fake punched me in the arm. "Don't do it again."

"I won't."

"Good." She looked at her husband. "Is Thane ready to go?"

"Yep. You want me to put him in the car seat?"

"Please."

"Where's Thane going?" I asked.

"Daycare. Come on, Spence. Let's put your shoes on. It's time to play with your friends."

"*Fwiends*," Spencer said and sprinted for the door. He came back five seconds later with his footwear.

Addison got down on the floor to help her son. "Maddox and Tommy are going to finish up the windows today, and the boys are going to daycare, so I thought you and I could go do something. Just the two of us."

"That...sounds great." I was confused as to why she wasn't yelling at me or at least telling me why she was disappointed in me.

I looked over at Tommy, and he shrugged, as if he knew what I was thinking.

Maybe he did.

Addison stood. "You have anything you want to do in particular?" she asked me.

I shook my head.

"Why don't you think about it while I run the kids to daycare? We can do anything you want, but tonight, the four of us are going out. Maddox's niece already agreed to babysit."

"Oh. I didn't bring anything for going out," I said.

She laughed. "We're in Brook Creek. Nobody dresses up here. But if you want, we can go shopping. Shopping is only twenty minutes away."

"I'll think about it."

"Sounds good. I'll be back in a few minutes."

23

TOMMY

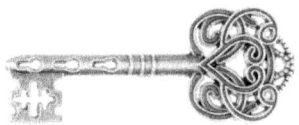

hile Maddox and I headed to the backyard, Olivia and Addison left to go to the next town over. It was nowhere near the size of Des Moines, but the next town did have the important amenities you wanted in a city, like a few clothing stores. It wasn't large enough to have a Home Depot or a Menards though, or Olivia and I could have saved a trip to Des Moines. But then, if we hadn't gone there, I never would have found out that Olivia was in trouble.

"So, did the police seem concerned?" Maddox asked.

"Not really. But I'm not all that surprised. She defends the people they arrest, and whoever is writing the letters hasn't done any physical harm to Olivia."

"If you need me to call the police chief, I will."

I raised my brow. "You're friends?"

Maddox laughed. "*Friends* is a very strong word. We are acquaintances."

Acquaintances was better than nothing.

"I'll let you know."

He wiped sweat off his forehead with the back of his hand. "*You'll* let me know?"

"Yes."

"Not Addison? Not Olivia herself?"

"You literally just said, 'If *you* need me to call the police chief.' Why are you acting like it's weird that I'd let you know?"

He grinned. "Maybe I was just waiting to see what you'd say."

I put my hands on my hips. "I don't follow."

Maddox jumped down into the window well. "Where'd you stay last night?"

"At Olivia's house." I lowered a window down to him.

"But where did you sleep?"

"In a bed." I hopped into the window well next to him.

He wiggled his eyebrows at me. "In Olivia's bed?"

"What are you, fifteen?" I picked up the new window while Maddox picked up the other, and we slowly set it in the frame we had already built.

"No," he answered. "Why won't you tell me?"

"Fine. I slept in her bed, all right?"

"Damn, man, you don't waste any time."

"Look at that. Maybe women aren't scared of me after all."

Maddox laughed but abruptly stopped. "You didn't take advantage of Olivia's vulnerable nature, did you?"

"Believe it or not, she came to me."

"You could have said no."

"No, you don't understand. She came to me on Wednesday night."

Maddox's eyebrows almost hit his hairline. "No shit?"

"No shit." I smirked. "Apparently, seeing you and

Addison having sex made her realize she'd been missing something. And I was the one she asked to help her."

He frowned. "Say that again?"

I started laughing. "Addison didn't tell you that Olivia caught you two in your living room? FYI, I'm never sitting on your couch again unless you plan to get it steam cleaned."

"No, Addison didn't tell me."

"Huh. Look at that. You two do keep things from each other."

"I'm going to kill her."

"Who? Olivia? Or Addison?"

"Addison. Why would I kill Olivia?"

"Why would you kill Addison?"

"Because she didn't tell me that her friend caught me fucking my wife."

I studied Maddox. "Are you embarrassed?"

He scowled at me. "Fuck no. I don't have anything to be embarrassed about."

I tilted my head.

He sighed. "Fine. I'm a little embarrassed. When I'm making love to my wife, I don't expect there to be an audience."

"Don't be embarrassed. It was so hot that she needed me to take the edge off."

I swore I could literally see his chest swell with pride.

"Ugh. Go get a room."

He looked around. "With who?"

"Yourself. You two make me sick."

"Us two?"

"Yeah. You and your ego."

Maddox rolled his eyes at my joke. "I'll get a room with my ego as soon as you do."

"Hmm." I gave it a thought. "That's fair."

"Ya think…*Flash*?"

"Whatever. Why don't you just get in your basement and make sure this window is in place, so we're not here all night?"

He braced himself on the edge of the well and jumped out. He turned and put his hand on my shoulder. "Just remember, no matter how good you think you are in bed, I'm better."

I swung to knock his arm off me, but he was already standing. I waited for him to get downstairs and face me in the window. When he gave me a thumbs-up, I gave him the finger.

24

OLIVIA

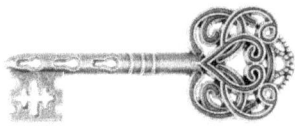

*A*ddison and I walked into the dark small-town bar and took two seats at the counter.

We had gotten back to Brook Creek about an hour ago. We'd picked up her kids from daycare but left as soon as Maddox's niece, Serena, showed up.

Tommy and Maddox had still been working in the backyard. They barely even acknowledged the two of us; they were so busy. So, Addison and I had changed clothes, refreshed our makeup, and come downtown. Brook Creek's downtown was so small that I would have less than a block to walk home after we called it quits tonight.

"What are you getting to drink?" Addison asked.

"I don't know. Why don't you pick? I can drink whatever because I don't have to drive."

"How about Southern Comfort and lemonade?"

"I've never had it."

Her eyes lit up. "You'll love it." She stood up on her barstool and leaned over the counter. "Hey, Wade, get your butt down here and serve us some drinks."

The bartender slapped the counter in front of him as he said good-bye to the patron he was speaking to and walked down to us.

"Ladies, what can I do for you?"

"Two SCs and lemonade, please."

Wade pulled out two glasses and started pouring. He glanced up at me. "That'll be five dollars for you." He pushed my drink over. "And, Addison, you owe me ten."

I almost choked on the sip I'd just taken. "Why is hers more?"

"Because she's bossy."

Addison slapped a ten on the bar. "He's kidding. It's five for both of us."

I pulled another five out of my purse. "Here's a tip for putting up with Addison."

"*Hey.*"

Wade and I both laughed.

"You want to get a table?" I asked her.

"Sure."

It was still rather early in the night, so we didn't have to fight for a table. But then again, maybe it was always this dead in a small town. I was only assuming it would get busier.

Addison and I talked about our day. Like the skirt and top I had found on sale, which I had opted to wear out tonight. But there was one subject I hadn't brought up all day, and now, with a little bit of alcohol in me, I figured it was about time.

"Why didn't you yell at me?"

Her brow furrowed. "Huh?"

"When I got to your house this morning, why didn't you yell at me? About the letters?"

"Oh, I wanted to, and I thought about it." She put her hand on mine from across the table. "Only because I love you and I'm scared." She pulled her arm away and took a sip of her drink. "But Tommy messaged me and said that you had already been through a lot, that you understood you'd messed up, and I shouldn't make you feel worse."

A fuzzy feeling warmed my chest. "Really?"

"Yep."

"That was nice of him." It was actually very sweet of him, but I didn't voice the thought.

Addison smiled. "Speak of the devil."

I was about to ask what she meant when Maddox appeared behind Addison and I felt what had to be Tommy behind me.

I turned to him. He looked like he'd just showered, and he smelled like it, too. Clean, fresh man scent.

"You smell good," I said as he pulled out the chair next to me.

He smiled. "Thanks." He leaned in close. "So do you."

"Did you guys finish the windows?" Addison asked as Maddox sat next to her.

"Yes."

"Oh, good. Then, we have the rest of the weekend to have fun."

"Speaking of fun"—Maddox got a glint in his eye that I sensed was trouble—"I heard that someone saw us having sex."

The bartender approached the table and placed two beers in front of Tommy and Maddox. They paid, and Wade walked away.

"Why didn't you tell me we gave Olivia a little show, Addy?"

She shrugged. "I knew she'd be embarrassed if you knew." She frowned. "But if I didn't tell you, then who did?"

"Tommy told me this afternoon."

Addison did a double take and looked at me. "You told *Tommy* you saw us?"

I shrugged. "I was traumatized. I needed to talk to someone about it," I joked.

"Traumatized? You said it was hot."

Maddox slowly turned his head. "Interesting. I mean, I knew we were hot, babe, but hearing someone else say that brings us to a whole new level."

Addison rolled her eyes.

"Of course, Olivia, you now owe us for the sex show. Addy and I don't perform for free."

Addison socked her husband in the stomach. "Leave Olivia alone." She shook her head. "I still can't believe you told Tommy." She wasn't mad, just surprised.

"If you want to be technical, he guessed that I saw you."

"Why would he guess that?"

Tommy put his hand on my leg, but it didn't stop me from answering. I smiled at Maddox. "Because your husband told Tommy to leave your house so that he could fuck his wife."

"I thought you didn't like that word?" Tommy asked.

"Hey, I'm practically quoting him. I don't want to get the words wrong."

"Maddox Wolfe, you actually tell people that you're going to fuck your wife?" Addison said.

He lifted a shoulder. "Not people. Just Tommy. And maybe a few others. But they're my friends." He yanked Addison's chair closer to his. "And don't pretend to be all mad. I hear you on the phone. Women talk about getting it as much as men."

Addison grinned and kissed Maddox. "I know, babe. I just like giving you shit."

He lowered his voice. "You're going to pay for that later."

"Ooh, I'm scared."

I turned to Tommy. "I can't believe you told Maddox that I saw him."

"I figured Addison had already done it."

"How did it come up anyway?" Addison asked.

"Uh…" Tommy said, looking like a deer in headlights.

"We were talking about you and him having sex," Maddox said.

Addison's head whipped around to me. "You and Tommy had sex?"

"Shh, not so loud." I tried to be serious, but I was laughing. "I was going to tell you. I just hadn't had time yet."

"We've been together all day."

"Okay, so it didn't come up. But I swear, I was going to."

Addison leaned in close. "Was it good?"

I leaned in, too. "He can hear you." I sat up. "I think I need another drink. This conversation is all over the place."

Wade seemed to show up out of thin air. "I come bearing gifts." He set four drinks on the table. "I noticed you were getting low."

"Thanks, Wade," Addison said.

"You're welcome."

"What do we owe you?" Tommy asked.

"Oh, this round is free. The four of you are the best entertainment I've had all week. If there are any more secrets to tell, keep them coming."

Wade walked away, and the four of us sat in silence for a minute, but then I opened my mouth and blurted out,

"Tommy and Maddox have had sex in front of each other. And once in the same bed."

Wade burst out laughing from behind the bar.

25

TOMMY

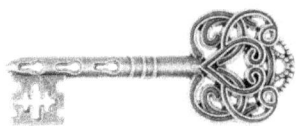

*A*ddison's mouth dropped, and then she surprised me because she started laughing. She put her hand on her stomach and fell into Maddox; she was laughing so hard.

She sat up after about thirty seconds. "Olivia, when Wade said to tell more secrets, he was joking."

"Oh." She picked up her glass and sipped. "Okay."

"How much have you had to drink?"

She grinned at me. "This is only my second one."

"You're going to be carrying her home," Maddox said to me.

"I haven't had that much to drink. I can walk just fine."

Maddox snorted. "Wade makes his drinks strong." He glanced at his wife. "You're not going to give me any crap about Olivia's latest reveal?" He then looked at me. "Thanks for keeping that to yourself, man."

"Hey, Olivia thought you'd be mad at her about the whole *catching you in the act* thing. I was trying to make her feel better. I was proving you wouldn't care."

"And it worked. But I'm still trying to picture it," Olivia said. "Didn't the women care?"

"It's not like we were putting on a show," I said. "There was usually a bed or blankets or something to cover up with. The other person just happened to be in the same room. And this was all when we were young. It hasn't happened in years."

"God, I hope not, or I'm missing something," Addison said.

"I meant, years before Maddox left the Teams."

Addison leaned over to her husband and put her hand between his legs. "I don't like the thought of you having sex with someone else."

Maddox put his hand on Addison's. "Baby, you know you're the only one for me."

"Good. And don't you forget it." She got up from her chair. "Meet me in the restroom. I need to talk to you about something."

I snorted. "That's what you're calling it now? *Talking*?"

Maddox lifted his arms in a dramatic shrug and went after his wife.

After the two of them were gone, Olivia turned to me. "Addison told me that you messaged her and asked her not to say anything about the letters. Thank you."

"You're welcome. I figured you were stressed out enough, and you didn't need to have someone add to it." I took a sip of my beer and noticed her outfit for the first time. "Did you have fun today? Are your clothes new?"

"I did have fun." She sat back and spread her arms. "And these clothes are new. *Everything* I'm wearing is new." She smiled and wiggled her eyebrows.

I laughed and pulled her to the edge of her chair. "What

if I told you I don't believe you and that I need to check to make sure you're not lying?"

She shifted her knees apart. "I'd say, go ahead."

I looked around, but I didn't have to worry. The sun was on its way down, so the tinted windows blocked most of the sunlight out. And the lighting was dark in the rest of the place. Also, since night was coming, more people had filed in, so I knew that the bartender was busy and wouldn't be paying attention to our table anymore.

I skimmed my hands up her thighs until I reached her hips, where I expected to find a thong or some other skimpy underwear, but all I met was bare skin.

I tugged her closer to me, so her knees were over my hips. "Olivia, are you naked under your skirt?"

She put her hand to her lips and pretended to be surprised. "Oh no, I did lie to you. It's not new. I was born with it."

"And what are we going to do about that?"

She smiled at me coyly. "What do you think we should do about it?"

"I have a few ideas."

I still hadn't brought out my purchases from the day before. After Olivia had received that letter at home, she'd been pretty shaken up. Last night wasn't the right time. She'd needed comfort. But tonight was different.

"Are you going to share with the rest of the class?"

"Nope. You're just going to have to wait to find out." I brushed a hand between her legs, and she sucked in a breath. "But I'll give you a hint. It has to do with this pretty pussy."

I gently pushed a lone digit inside her. She grasped the table and moaned.

I loved how she responded to me. For someone who had

been so rigid the first time I met her, she had really opened up to me.

I teased her a bit, not sure how far I wanted to take this in the bar.

"I feel like you're always touching me, and I never touch you. I never get you off. It's not fair," Olivia said.

My dick jumped in my pants, obviously liking the idea of Olivia touching him. "That's okay. It's not like I don't have any fun when we're together."

"No, it's not okay. I want to make you feel good the way you make me feel good."

"You do." I withdrew my hand from her body and pulled her, so she was straddling my lap. I kissed her and pushed my erection into her crotch. "See how good you make me feel? Can you tell how hard I am for you?"

She smiled. "You are actually proving my point, you know. You're showing me that you're turned on, but I'm not doing anything about it. I'm not taking care of you."

I should have known not to argue with a lawyer. "We'll do something about it later. When we're alone."

She pulled at her skirt, fanning it around us. "Or we could do something about it now."

Before I could fully process her statement, she was unbuttoning my jeans and unzipping my fly. She pulled my cock out and rubbed her sweet cleft over it.

I stilled her hips. "You're going to torture me like this. It's going to be a long night if you leave me with blue balls."

"Move over to my seat by the wall," she suggested.

I realized listening to her might be an unwise move, but I picked her up and moved over anyway. A few people looked, as the movement must have caught their eye, but they turned away, uninterested.

Now, with the two of us in her chair, she reached between us again, pulled out my cock, and drew me into her body.

Stunned, I hugged her to me and shuddered. She was wet and hot and so tight that I thought I got light-headed for a minute.

"I can't believe you just did that," I said to her.

She leaned back, so I could see her face. "Why?"

"Because we're in a room full of people."

"Who think we're talking while I'm sitting on your lap. There's no crime in that."

"I think I might be a little bit of an exhibitionist because I am turned on as fuck."

"Hmm…"

She rotated her pelvis a little while putting the most bored expression on her face. If she wasn't so wet, I would think she could not care less about being on my lap.

"Is this how you win cases?" I asked.

She kept up her minuscule rocking. "What do you mean?"

"Your face says you'd rather be anywhere but here, yet your pussy is saying otherwise."

A tiny smile spread across her face. "I suppose I've perfected my body language for court. Juries can be influenced by subtle things."

"Yeah? Well, right now, my dick is influenced by how wet you are."

She shook out her hair behind her back. "I do have to say, you feel incredible inside me."

My cock jumped.

"Oh. I liked that."

"Talk dirty again," I ordered.

She smiled. "I want to feel you come inside me."

"That will do it." I yanked her close, not caring if anyone thought they saw what they saw. I put my hands on her hips and directed her movements the way I knew would make us both feel the best. They weren't big or wild, but they were enough that I was going to bring us both to climax. "Keep fucking me just like that. I want to come inside you. I want to fill you up so that you feel me the rest of the night." I leaned back in my chair and arched my back, so her clit could rub against my pelvis with her every move. "Just like that, baby. I want you to come all over me."

Olivia's body stiffened, and she squeezed her eyes shut. She looked like she was in pain. But deep in her center, where I was connected to her, she pulsed and contracted around me. I held on as long as I could, wanting to enjoy the feel of her coming, but soon, I was a goner, too.

I dropped my head over the back of my chair and stared up at the dingy ceiling as I exploded and emptied myself inside her.

I lay like that for about a minute or so to control my breathing. I didn't want it to look like I'd just run a marathon and give away what the two of us had just done in a room full of people.

I chuckled as I realized that we'd just had sex in public.

"You okay?" she asked.

I grinned and lifted my head. "Fuck yeah. You?"

She chuckled. "I can't believe I just did that, but yes." She looked down at our bodies. Her skirt still covered us well, and no one would know that I was still inside her.

"Hey, what are you two doing?" a feminine voice asked.

Olivia looked over her shoulder, and I peeked around her. Addison and Maddox were back.

"Talking," I said.

It wasn't a lie.

She narrowed her eyes. "You sure? You two look pretty intimate over there."

Olivia and I both laughed. She slowly stood over me, her skirt still covering me.

I quickly shoved my dick in my pants and buttoned up.

She swung her leg over and sat down in my chair. "Is the restroom safe to use now that you two aren't in it?"

Maddox and Addison exchanged looks.

Addison shrugged. "It's always been safe."

"Right," I said, my voice full of skepticism.

I exchanged looks with Olivia. Not that it was much safer out here.

26

OLIVIA

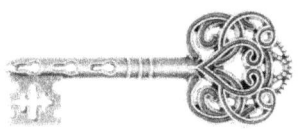

Tommy and Maddox went off to shoot pool, leaving Addison and me sitting alone.

I moved back to my chair, so I could lean against the wall and put my feet up on Tommy's chair. With alcohol in my system and my blood pressure lowered, thanks to a spectacular orgasm, I was relaxed and feeling good.

"I've been thinking," Addison said.

I rolled my head against the wall, so I could see her. She looked nervous.

"About what?" I asked.

"I think Tommy should go back to Des Moines with you when your stay here is over."

I dropped my feet to the floor and sat up, relaxed feeling over. "What?"

"I'm worried about you. You're a single woman who lives by yourself. What if something happens to you?" She shook her head. "I could never live with myself if I didn't try to do something to keep you safe. Tommy isn't working right now. He planned to stay here for a month to help Maddox with the house, but now that the windows are done, that can wait."

I tried to imagine what it would be like to have Tommy come home with me.

While he had stayed the night and we'd spent a lot of time together, could I handle him practically living with me?

More importantly, could I handle the feeling I had right now—that I liked the idea of him living with me?

What happened when he went back to Virginia? Or worse, what happened if we got sick of each other?

I was really enjoying being with him, but it wasn't permanent.

I wasn't going to say no outright because I didn't want Addison to worry, and I had to admit, I would feel safer with Tommy around.

It just wasn't a simple thing to say yes or no to.

"I'll think about it," I told her.

"I was hoping for a yes, but I'll take it." She leaned closer to me. "Between you and me, this would be something good for Tommy, too. I think he's a little lost now that he retired from the Navy. I saw Maddox struggle with it. It's hard to go from having a job that you feel is making a difference to not doing anything."

I raised my eyebrows. "So, I'd be doing this for Tommy?"

She grinned. "If that's the way you want to look at it, then yes."

I laughed. "We need to really try a case together again. I'd love to see you at work in court."

She chuckled. "Thanks. I like to think I haven't lost all the skills I learned in school while working here in Brook Creek." Her smile slipped from her face, and her eyes turned concerning. "Please think about it for real though, okay?"

I nodded. "I will. But it's not all up to me. Tommy has to be on board with it. And I don't want him to do it because he has to even if you think it would be good for me. There are other things I can do to make my place safer."

Addison sat up straight. "You're right. Let's ask him." She raised her arm in the air and waved. "Tommy," she yelled out.

I shook my head and hissed, "Not now."

She lowered her arm. "Why not? Now's perfect."

Tommy and Maddox walked back to our table, and I groaned.

"What's up?" Tommy asked.

"I'm worried about Olivia when she goes back home. I know you planned to stay in Iowa for a few more weeks. What if you went back with her to keep her safe until the police find who's been sending the letters? I'm sure Maddox wouldn't mind putting off the work on the house."

"Of course not, babe," Maddox said. "Olivia's safety comes first."

I turned around in my seat and met Tommy's eyes. "You don't have to come back with me. You didn't come here to be with me, you came to be with your friend, and I don't want to hog all your time."

I held my breath, waiting to see what he had to say.

"When do you plan to go home?"

"Tuesday. I was planning to be here a week. Unless something comes up," I had to add because something could always come up. I was already feeling guilty about staying that late. I should be working on Tate's new case.

"Why don't we see what happens after this weekend? Maybe the police will find something before Tuesday."

For some reason, this was the perfect response. If he had

said no, I thought my feelings would have been hurt, but if he had said yes, I thought I'd be uncomfortable. We didn't know each other that well, and if he jumped at the chance to stay with me for a few weeks, I'd think something was wrong with him.

I am a hard woman to please.

I laughed out loud at my thought because it was so true.

"What's so funny?" Addison asked.

I shook my head. "Nothing. Just thinking about how fickle I am."

"Kind of out of the blue, but I'm not going to argue."

"Ha-ha," I said sarcastically.

I turned around to the guys, only to see that they had already returned to their pool game.

"You like him, don't you?"

I looked back at my friend. "He has a certain appeal."

"Yes." She clenched her fist in victory. "I knew it." She smiled. "He's good in bed, isn't he?"

I closed my eyes and shook my head. "Oh, Addison."

"What?"

"You make me laugh."

"Just tell me."

"Yes, he's good in bed."

She patted herself on the back...literally. "Chalk that up to another thing I'm right about."

I rolled my eyes.

"Now, tell me how you two ended up in bed together."

"Fine," I said even though I was dying to tell her everything. I put my elbows on the table. "I have you and the window you uncovered to thank."

27

TOMMY

*I*t was getting late, and the bar was closing in about an hour. "Is it time for us to leave yet?" I asked. "I'm starting to feel real old with all these young kids out."

I didn't often feel thirty-eight, but being around a bunch of young twenty-something kids made me feel every bit of my age.

"I'm ready to go, too," Addison said. "Serena is probably wondering when we're going to get home." She groaned. "Tomorrow morning is going to suck. Just once, it would be nice if the boys slept in."

Maddox put his arm around her. "We'll take turns, so both of us can sleep. I'll take the first shift."

She kissed him. "God bless good husbands."

The four of us finished our drinks and strode out into the warm night air. As we walked out, Addison stumbled against Maddox.

"Oops," she said with a laugh.

"Are you sure either of you should be driving?" I asked.

"It would look really bad if the sheriff got pulled over for driving drunk."

Maddox slid his arm around his wife's waist. "We'll probably walk."

Addison sighed. "But I'm so tired. Carry me home."

Maddox laughed. "I don't think so."

"Why don't you go and sleep at Addison's old place?" I smiled and put my arm across Olivia's shoulders. "I have it on good authority that the sheets are clean and have never been used."

I couldn't be positive, but I thought Olivia turned red under the streetlights.

Addison gasped. "Never been used, huh? The first night, Liv? That's awesome." She turned and faced Maddox, throwing her arms around his neck. "It'll be like old times. Before we had kids and you used to sneak into my room." She kissed his jaw. "Please."

"I need to ask Serena if it's okay," he said, pulling his phone out of his pocket.

"We'll be at my place, whatever you two decide." I swung Olivia around to head to my place. "See you tomorrow." I put my hand up in a wave.

"That's pretty presumptuous of you to think I'm coming home with you," Olivia pointed out once we were out of earshot.

"Nah. You and I both know it's the truth."

"We do?"

"Yeah. You can't think after what happened in the bar that we're done for the night. I have plans for you."

She sucked in a breath and shuddered against me. "You sure know how to entice a lady."

I laughed. "Oh, I know how to do much more than that."

When we got to my place, I walked her upstairs without an argument because I had been right. She'd always been planning to go home with me the whole time.

The second we walked in the door, I pushed her up against the wall and kissed her. I loved how she opened up for me and let me thrust my tongue into her mouth, as if it belonged there. I continued to kiss her—sometimes gently, sometimes with more vigor—as I stripped us both.

I growled and raised one of her knees up and back toward the wall, opening her completely. I pushed two fingers into her. "Yes. Still so wet and full from me." I slid my digits out and rubbed it against her clit.

She moaned.

"Let's go to the bedroom." I picked her up and carried her to the mattress, where I laid her down. "Stay right there," I said, turning on the lamp sitting on the nightstand.

As I went over to the corner of the room to pick up the black plastic bag of stuff I had bought the other morning, I noticed she had lifted her head and was watching me. I brought my purchases over to the bed and tipped the bag over to empty it.

"What is all that?" she asked.

I held up some black rope. "This is a rope specifically made for tying someone up. It's made of satin, so it won't scratch the skin." I walked over to the head of the bed and picked up one of her arms. When she didn't pull away or object, I said, "Let me demonstrate." As I gently tied her wrist to the headboard, I asked, "Have you ever been tied up?"

She nodded. "Once."

I paused, amazed. "Didn't expect you to say that." Olivia had some surprises apparently. I walked around to the other side and began working on the other arm. "Did you like it?"

"Not really." She raised a shoulder. "But I didn't hate it. I just didn't care for it."

"More indifferent?" I asked.

"Yes."

"Well, I'm going to make sure you love it."

She laughed. "You can try."

I laughed, too. I was going to do more than try.

I got onto the bed and straddled her upper body. I took note of how close my dick was to her face, but it wasn't the time for that. I needed her to feel safe with me first.

I took each binding and waved the end of the rope, so she could see them. "If at any time this is too much for you and you can't wait for me to free you, pull these, and it will release you. Okay?"

She nodded.

Seeing as she understood, I put each end in her hands and explained, "This way, you don't have to search for them."

I got off the bed, and I thought she made a sound of disappointment.

I smiled to myself. I was hoping she would appreciate the buildup.

I went to my pile at the end of the bed. "Also, you need a safe word in case you want me to stop or help you."

"What's the word?"

"What do you want it to be? It has to be something we wouldn't say during sex. Something like food or a random object."

She appeared to think on it. After a few seconds, she smiled. "Flynn Bass."

I started laughing. "That's a good one. It will definitely be a *what the fuck* moment if I hear you say that. Flynn Bass it is."

I bent both of her legs as I knelt by her ass and splayed her wide.

I liked the safe word, but I needed her to understand something. "For the record, Olivia, I know I like to joke a lot and have fun, but if you ever say another man's name while you're in my bed, neither of us is going to be happy. While you're here with me, you're mine. I don't share. Is that understood?"

I stared at her, waiting for her to answer. I needed her to know I was serious about this.

She swallowed and nodded.

I smiled. "Good." I reached over to my pile and picked up two different items.

"What are those?" she asked.

I raised my right hand higher, so she could see better. "This one is for your clitoris. I know it's hard for you to have an orgasm during sex because you need your clit stimulated. I want to work on your G-spot while I work your clit. The more you associate your G-spot pleasure with the pleasure you get from your clit, the more likely you can come from having sex with just my cock."

Her eyes enlarged. "Does that really work?"

"Sometimes, yes, and sometimes, no." I wanted to be honest. "But we'll have fun trying. Unfortunately, it's going to take more than a few days." Days we didn't have. "You can buy a vibrator for just your G-spot to keep working on it after you go back home, so you don't lose any progress we make while together."

I didn't like the thought of her using toys when I

wouldn't get to be there. I was already jealous, and it made me want to tell her I was going back with her, no matter what. But if she was out of harm's way, I didn't think she'd take too kindly to me invading her life or her space.

"And the other one?" she asked.

I held up my left arm. "This is an anal vibrator."

She raised her eyebrows and then wrinkled her nose.

"Why?" was the only thing that came out of her mouth.

I laughed again.

"I know what butt plugs and anal beads are," she explained. "But I've never heard of a vibrator for the ass."

"People use it for the same reason you'd put one in your vagina. Because it feels good."

"If you say so," she said skeptically.

I dropped my hands to my waist as a realization came to me. "Have you never had anal sex?"

"No."

I tilted my head back and sighed as I focused my thoughts. When I looked at her again, I said, "Fuck, do I want to be your first." I wanted it so badly.

"What if you hurt me? You're not small."

"I thank you for the kind words, but I would make sure you were very prepared. And we'd probably have to build up to my dick." My erection jumped, and it was so hard, it ached. I shook my head rapidly. "I have to stop thinking about it, or I'm going to fricking come like a teenager all over your stomach." I set the anal vibrator down. "We'll save that one for later."

Hopefully, not too much later.

28

OLIVIA

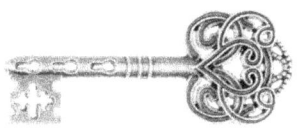

Tommy grabbed an empty pillow from beside my head and pushed it under my hips. I had to admit, I was very curious as to what he had planned for me and why I needed to be tied up for it.

"Nervous?" he asked.

"No. More like curious."

"Good."

He put down the other vibrator and climbed over me. First, he kissed me slow and deep while his hands roamed my body. I didn't know how long this went on. Only that my lips were swollen, and I was feeling light-headed.

He moved down south, kissing, licking, and sucking on each nipple. Several times, I tried to touch him, only to be stopped short by the ropes keeping me tied to the bed.

"You're doing that thing again," I complained.

He lifted his head. "What thing?"

"The thing where you're giving me all the pleasure. I want to make you feel good."

The corner of his mouth tipped up. "Oh, trust me. Seeing you lying here for me to feast on gives me great pleasure."

"I want to touch you."

"Soon."

Thomas Morelli was a lying liar because I did not get to touch him soon.

When he was finished with my breasts, he kissed his way down my pelvis. He sucked on the inside of my thighs and had me squirming beneath him as he ignored my spread legs and what I was offering between them.

Finally, he stopped messing around and turned his gaze to my center. He swiped his fingers over my lips and held up his hand. "You know, I actually bought lube, but I should have known it would be a waste of money. I have never seen another woman as wet as you."

I clicked my tongue, and he laughed.

"That's a fucking compliment, Liv." He rubbed his fingers over my labia and circled my clit. "All this wetness…just for me."

Without warning, two fingers were pushed inside me, and I gasped.

Tommy rubbed the anterior part of my vagina until he got to the spot that made me squirm. "Feel good?"

"Yes."

"Think you can come this way?"

I paused but shook my head. "No."

"Let's find out, shall we?"

He continued to work the spot, and it felt good, but I wasn't going to have an orgasm. I was about to tell him the bad news when he wrapped his lips around my clit and sucked.

My back arched off the bed, and I pulled on my bindings.

There was almost a freedom in being tied up. I could move as much as I wanted, and I knew that I wasn't going anywhere.

Tommy looked up and met my eyes. He didn't turn away as he pushed the base of his tongue against my clit and rubbed.

I had never had a guy make eye contact with me as they went down on me like this. It was sexy as hell.

The tingling in my pelvis started, signaling that my orgasm was coming soon. I tried to give him a look that said, *Don't stop.*

Just when I was sure I was about to crash over the edge, he lifted his head. I was ready to cry out in defeat, but he jerked his fingers inside me up and down, and instead of igniting from my clit out, I exploded from my G-spot.

My whole body shook all the way to my fingers and toes.

I gasped for air as waves upon waves of bliss washed over me.

I was still twitching after a minute, but I had calmed down enough to gather my thoughts.

Tommy sat up and knelt between my legs once more. "Let's try that again, shall we?"

I could feel my eyes widen. "I don't think I can do that again."

He smiled. "Won't know until you try." He took himself in his hand and rubbed his cock all over my slit and then slowly sank inside me.

"Oh God," I said. With my hips at an angle, it was like he was touching all new corners of me that I hadn't known existed.

But most of all, I felt him touch my G-spot. It was sensitive, and while I couldn't be sure, I swore it was swollen.

"Fuck. For someone who just came, you sure are tight."

I clenched my muscles around him.

"Hey. None of that. I have work to do."

I was about to ask him what when he grabbed the clit vibrator. I heard the hum of the motor as he turned it on. And when he put it between my legs, I would have bucked him off me if I wasn't tied up or he were a weaker man.

"Holy shit, I'm sensitive." I was surprised since he had stopped touching me there before I had my orgasm.

"I'll put it on the lowest setting, but if it's too much, let me know. And don't forget the safe word."

I nodded.

This time, I was prepared, and even though it was still a jolt to the system, I managed to stay in one place.

Tommy began thrusting as he rubbed the vibrator on me. His movements were slow and unhurried at first. But as my arousal was climbing again, he picked up his speed. After several minutes, I made plans to steal the vibrator from him if he didn't give it to me.

But like before, when I was on the edge of coming, he turned off the vibrator and threw it across the room. He grabbed on to my hips and literally slid me across his cock over and over again.

And when I actually felt pain deep inside of me, an orgasm roared toward me like a freight train. I was only aware of the white-hot feeling that flushed over my body, and then everything went black.

———

I slowly lifted my eyelids, blinking once or twice as I scanned the mostly dark room. My arms were untied, and I was cuddled up to an incredible warmth.

"Tommy."

He ran his hands over my head. "Yeah?"

"Am I alive?" I joked.

He laughed. A full-belly laugh that had him rolling onto his back. After a minute, he wiped the tears from his eyes and squeezed my side. "Yeah, you're alive."

"Did I pass out?" I asked seriously this time.

He brushed his thumb back and forth over my cheek. "Yeah. Scared the hell out of me."

"How long was I out?"

"Maybe thirty seconds. I untied you right away, took you into my arms, and turned off the light in case it was too bright for you."

"Did you come?"

"Uh, *no*. I like my woman awake and consenting, thank you very much."

"Good," I said as I searched for his penis. It immediately grew hard in my hand, just the way I'd wanted it to.

"Good?" He groaned. "I give you an orgasm so good that you pass out, and you're happy that I didn't get one at all?"

I chuckled. "No, big guy. I'm saying good because I get to do this." I pulled the covers over my head and slithered down the bed.

29

TOMMY

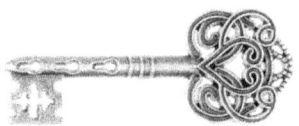

It was my turn to almost pass out as Olivia sucked on the head of my dick. *Holy shit*. And I'd thought her pussy felt good. I mean, it did. Don't get me wrong. There was just something about a woman's mouth that felt amazing.

I flipped the covers off her head, so I could watch her take me. It was dark in the room, but my eyes had adjusted enough, so I had a decent view. I couldn't wait to see what Olivia would do with her mouth.

I didn't care if she had the skills of an amateur or if she had blown the whole hockey team in high school. No matter what she did, it was bound to feel great.

She twirled her tongue around my crown and placed sucking kisses down the side of my cock from the tip to the root and then back up again on the opposite side.

She placed me on the edge of her lips and sucked me down.

I groaned and tried to keep my hips from bucking.

Olivia got up on her hands and knees and slowly bobbed

her head. The thrusting combined with suction had me closing my eyes and trying to fight off my orgasm. It was all going to end way too soon.

I felt the tightening in my nuts, as there was a sudden change in the way her mouth felt.

I lifted my head to look down my body while Olivia cupped my balls and pushed her nose to my groin as she took me in all the way. All it took was her swallowing once, causing everything to tighten as she deep-throated me, and I was gone.

I tried to warn her I was going to come, but an incoherent sound came out instead.

I could do nothing but lie there as Olivia drank all of me down, and my climax went on and on.

And if that wasn't the sexiest fucking thing ever, I didn't know what was.

She slowly pulled me from her mouth and kissed her way up my body. When we were face-to-face, I cupped the back of her head and kissed her deep, taking my time now that I was completely sated.

I rolled Olivia off my body and tucked her against my side. "Thank you. That felt incredible."

She kissed my pec. "You're welcome."

I didn't know if I was going to screw things up by bringing up the subject of me going home with her, but I needed to tell her how I felt.

"Listen, about me going back to Des Moines with you, I really don't mind. If you haven't noticed, I don't have anything tying me to anywhere at the moment. I've been doing temporary jobs lately, and I finished my last one less than a month ago."

"Why did you retire? You seem to have really liked the Navy."

I snorted. "Liked it? No, I loved it." I ran my hand over my face and sighed. "Unfortunately, my body couldn't handle it anymore. I injured my knee a few years back. The doctor told me to take it easy, or I was going to need a knee replacement before I was forty-five. But I took medical leave and healed right up." I chuckled. "Or so I thought. Turns out, all it took was jumping out of the back of a truck and landing on a rock to finish the fucking thing off. Thankfully, we were training and not on a mission because I couldn't even walk."

I had felt like the biggest pussy in front of my teammates that day. I hated thinking about how weak I'd looked to them. But when no one had given me shit, I had known it was serious.

"I saw the scar."

"Yeah. Turns out, the doctor was right because I got a new knee at thirty-eight." I lifted my leg, but the scar was hard to see in the dark. "And it feels great. I can walk, I can run"—I nuzzled Olivia's temple—"and I can fuck you like you deserve. But it's too risky for missions. I would never be able to live with myself if someone got hurt or died because my body had failed me. So, here I am."

She sat up, and I watched the sheet fall from her small breasts. I never knew how much I liked them little until I saw Olivia's. Perky and still enough for me to suck on.

She ran her hand down my chest. "I'm sorry."

"What for?" I tugged her close and drew a nipple into my mouth. "They taste good, too," I muttered.

"What?"

I smiled. "Nothing. Talking to myself." I sucked on her dark bud again.

"Tommy?"

"Hmm?" I hummed around her nipple.

"If I need your help, I would be very grateful if you came home with me."

I released her with a pop. "Really?"

"Yes, but I feel like you're going to be awfully bored. I work a lot, and I don't do anything fun. You're going to want to go home after the first day. You could always look for something to do while you're in Des Moines."

I frowned. "But I'll be there to take care of you. I mean, watch over you."

"But I'll be at the office most of the time."

"Then, that's where I'll be."

"But you'll have to sit out in the waiting room. Attorney-client privilege."

"Is Derek excluded from everything?"

"No, but he works for me. I need his help, and he signed a contract with the firm."

"So, hire me to work for you."

She laughed. "It's not that easy. I don't have a position for you. And before you say bodyguard, that doesn't fall under attorney-client privilege."

"You'll figure it out."

She raised her eyebrows. "*I'll* figure it out?"

"Yeah. You're smart. Therefore, *you'll* figure it out." I ran my thumb over her other nipple. "But until then, I want you to know, you're plenty fun."

"Me or my breasts?" she asked suspiciously.

I sucked a tip in my mouth and swirled my tongue around it. "Both." I pulled her body over mine and rocked my shaft against her pelvic bone. "Open for me."

Her legs slid to my sides. "You're insatiable," she said against my lips.

Only for you, I thought as I pushed my cock inside her.

30

OLIVIA

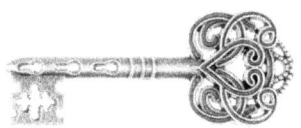

I blinked open my eyes and took in my surroundings. I was in Tommy's room in Maddox's old apartment, facing the wall.

This was the second time I'd woken up here, but unlike the first time, I had no desire to move from the warmth of Tommy's arms.

I rolled over slowly so as not to wake him, but I should have known that would be impossible to do.

"What are you doing?" he asked without opening his eyes. His voice was rough and sounded sexy from sleep.

"Looking at you."

"Do you like what you see?"

"Meh. It's okay."

He laughed but didn't say more, and within seconds, I was pretty sure he'd gone back to sleep.

I scanned his face. I'd never noticed how long his dark eyelashes were until now. Some women paid good money for eyelashes like that, and it just wasn't fair to waste it on a man who probably could not care less.

Tommy's face had a good amount of stubble this morning, and I kind of liked it. I wondered if he'd keep it if I told him not to shave. Above the facial hair were a couple of striking cheekbones, which I'd also never paid that close of attention to.

I thought it was because when Tommy was awake, there was so much of him. Not just his body, but his presence also, and certain features got lost in the whole package.

He really was a gorgeous specimen of a man.

I closed my eyes and considered going back to sleep when I noticed a warmth on my face. Something about this made me lift my lids again, and I looked around.

The brightness was the same as it had been before, so I didn't understand what had made me hyperaware of the situation.

I was halfway to thinking I was crazy when it hit me.

I gasped and sat up. "Tommy."

I must have startled him because he flew up and out of the bed, naked. "What's wrong? Is someone trying to break in?"

I pointed behind him. "The window."

He spun and sprinted over. He felt all around the seam and turned back to me. "It's fine. It's locked."

"It's open."

He hit his thumb against the glass a couple of times. "No, sweetheart, it's not."

I ground my teeth together. "I meant, the shade," I said as I gestured with my whole arm. "The shade is open."

He stared at me blankly.

"The shade is up. We had sex last night with the lights on." I flopped back on the bed and covered my head. I was never going to be able to face Addison and Maddox again. Especially Maddox.

Although…just because the shade hadn't been drawn, that didn't mean the two of them had looked through the window. They had probably been too busy having their own sex.

The comforter was slowly pulled out of my hands and lowered from my face.

Tommy stood over me with an amused grin on his face. "Care to share with the rest of the class?"

I shook my head. If I told him, he'd want to know how I knew.

He sat down next to me. "Come on. It can't be that bad."

"Addison used to have a bookcase that sat in front of the window in her apartment, but she took it with her when she moved."

"Okay."

I sighed and went for it. "And it looks into your place. How did you not notice?"

Good one, Olivia. Distract him with a question.

Tommy got up and walked back to look outside. "Hmm. So it does. I guess I never took the time to pay attention." He whirled around. "But it seems like someone has." His eyes were sparkling with humor.

"I only know because Addison warned me that she had taken the bookshelf."

He sauntered over to me and rubbed his chin. "Something tells me you're not speaking the whole truth."

I pushed the covers off and stood. "I need to shower. We have Brook Days today. We wouldn't want to keep the locals waiting."

Tommy snagged me in his arms and grinned at me. "You spied on me, didn't you?"

"*Spied* is a strong word. More like accidentally saw you as I was walking by."

"And did you keep walking?"

I looked around, not meeting his eyes. "No."

"So, you spied on me." He ran his nose along my neck. "What was I doing? And how did I not see you?"

"You don't pay attention, remember?"

"Oh, baby, I pay plenty of attention when it comes to you." He hiked me up higher so that my cleft rubbed against his now-hard cock.

I sighed. "My place was dark. You had the lights on and were undressing." I arched my neck, so he had better access. "I'm only human," I confessed.

"Was this before you came over to me that first night?"

"Yes."

My back hit cold glass, and I squeaked. "What are you doing?"

"Giving Maddox and Addison a show," he said, setting my butt on the edge of the windowsill.

"What?" I tried to squirm out of his embrace.

He threw his head back and laughed. "Relax. They didn't even stay at Addison's place last night."

I stopped trying to escape his embrace. "And you know this how?"

"He texted me last night. They felt bad because they're going to have someone watch the boys today, too." He pushed my legs open. "Now, let me in, and let's pretend like we're giving the neighbors a show."

31

TOMMY

"I wasn't expecting such a big crowd," I said, looking around. I was surprised to see how many people were here for Brook Days.

"We often have people come from out of town to celebrate. A lot of the residents invite family and friends."

"I wish you had told me about the chili cook-off. I make some great chili."

Olivia looked up at me in surprise. "You do?"

"Sorry, man. I haven't had it for so long; I forgot to tell you about it," Maddox said.

"It's fine," I told him. "I would have had to do a lot of preparing for it." I looked down at Olivia. "And, yes, I do. Maybe, someday, I'll make it for you. Unless you don't like it."

"No, I do."

"Can you handle spicy?"

She looked insulted. "Of course I can."

I smiled. "Okay. Extra-spicy chili coming your way. Someday."

"I look forward to it," Olivia said to me and turned to our friends. "So, what do you two usually do when you're here?" she asked Maddox and Addison.

"Maddox always plays flag football."

"Count me in for that," I said.

"There's also a baseball game or two."

I shook my head.

"And there are a lot of smaller games. Like horseshoes, mini-golf, and a three-legged race. The big bouncy house is for kids, but you're more than welcome to jump in," Maddox said.

"After you," I said.

The four of us walked around when we came across an event about to start soon.

"Oh, I want to do the three-legged race," Addison said.

"Sounds semi-fun," Maddox said.

"Not with you. You're way too tall. I meant, with Olivia."

Olivia smiled. "Let's do it. Do we get anything if we win?"

"I think we all get a prize when we're done whether we win or lose, but it's probably a kid prize."

"Nuts. I was hoping for some healthy competition."

"Maddox, why don't you and Tommy race against us?" Addison asked.

"Because it wouldn't be fair."

"How so?" she asked her husband.

"Flash and I worked together for years. We had to learn each other's body language. When we were on missions, we were in sync. The two of us together are like a well-oiled machine."

"*Please.*" Addison rolled her eyes.

"Yeah, that sounds like a bunch of BS that's code for *I don't want people to see me fall flat on my face*," Olivia said.

I laughed at Maddox's less than impressed face. "Look, I mean, Mad Dog has a point. I don't think you want to take us on."

Addison looked at Olivia. "They're calling each other by their stupid nicknames, as if that's supposed to intimidate us."

"Fine," Maddox said. "We'll race you."

Addison clapped her hands. "Yay."

"But we're going to bet on it. If you and Olivia lose, you two have to do something for Flash and me. And if you win, vice versa."

"How about losers make dinner tonight?" Addison suggested.

Olivia shook her head. "That's not good enough. We already know that Tommy can cook. It has to be something they don't want to do."

"Not if we did naked butlers."

Olivia pointed at Addison. "I like the way you think."

Maddox swung his arm between the two women. "What the hell are naked butlers, and how do you know about them?" He directed the last part of his question at his wife.

"I'm married, not dead, Maddox." She patted his arm. "Don't worry. I've never seen any in real life."

"Which is why this would be fun," Olivia added.

"You still haven't told us what they are," I said.

"In addition to cooking, you will wait on Olivia and me all night. But you only get to wear an apron and a bow tie."

"Don't forget the cuffs," Olivia said.

"Yeah, because that's the important piece of clothing to

put on while our asses are literally hanging out," Maddox said.

"Hey, it completes the outfit," Addison said.

"No deal," he said.

She stuck out her lower lip. "Boo. You're no fun."

"Too bad. Pick something else."

"Fine." Addison smiled. "You have to paint our toenails then."

I grimaced. I had baseball mitts for hands. There was no way I was going to be able to paint toenails and not look like an idiot. "I think I'd rather do the naked—"

Maddox stopped me with an arm to my abdomen. "Deal."

I threw my hands up in the air.

"Sorry," he said to me.

I scoffed, "No, you're not."

"What are we doing if you win?" Addison asked.

"You two have to give us massages," I butted in before Maddox could reply. I gave him a *see how you like it* look.

"Joke's on you because a massage sounds amazing," he told me.

"Addison, are you sure about this?" Olivia said. "They're communicating without even talking. And they're closer in height than the two of us."

"We'll be okay," Addison said. She put her hand up in front of her mouth and whispered, "Besides, if we lose, we'll hire a couple of masseuses to do the massages."

"No way," I said. "It has to be you two."

"Fine," she said.

"Shake on it."

The four of us shook hands, and after waiting for a few

minutes, we were handed ropes and told to line up at the starting line.

"We got this," Maddox said as he tied our ankles and I tied our thighs. "Just pretend we're out in the field and our lives depend on it." He moved up to our knees to tie us together there, too.

"Our lives don't depend on it, but our manhood just might."

Maddox stood and held out his fist.

I bumped it with my own. "Game on."

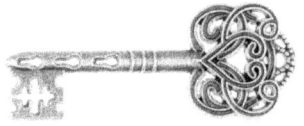

"*W*e're going to lose," I said as Addison and I tied our legs together. "They're trained professionals. You and I trained in a classroom."

"Don't worry. I have a plan."

"And what is that?" I didn't believe she had a good plan.

Addison pulled her shirt over her head and dropped it to the ground, leaving her in a white cami. She adjusted her breasts in her bra and pinched her nipples. Then, she rolled up her shorts, so they were basically underwear. She looked at me. "What are you doing? Start fixing your clothes, so you look sexy."

I stared at her. "This is never going to work. Men are not that dumb."

She snorted. "They are controlled by their dicks."

"That's not a nice thing to say about your husband."

"If the shoe fits. Besides I love him and his dick. And if it helps us win, then who am I to complain?"

I shook my head in disbelief. "Okay, but I think we're going to look like fools."

I had picked a summer dress with buttons in the front to wear, so I unbuttoned all four buttons and adjusted my own boobs. Mine weren't as big as Addison's, but I gave myself as much cleavage as I could manage.

Once that was done, I had to figure out how to show off my bottom half a little more.

"Tie the hem across your upper legs. If the guys ask, say you want to keep it out of the way."

I pulled the bottom of my dress to my side and tied it. "How's that?"

She gave me a thumbs-up. "Perfect."

I turned to see what the guys thought, but Addison pulled my arm. "Don't look yet. We have to wait to get their attention right before the race starts." She peeked over my shoulder. "They have their heads together and are talking. They won't be prepared for us."

"I still don't think they'll be affected."

Addison sighed. "Ye of little faith. Just look their way right before we hear *go* and give Tommy a look that says you're going to fuck his brains out later."

I wrinkled my nose. "I don't think I can manage a sexy look."

"You can if you believe it. Think sexy thoughts. And then think how fun it'll be to watch that big man paint your toenails."

"I really do want to see that. Okay, I will give it my all." Even though I thought this was a ridiculous plan.

Someone clapped their hands, and we all turned our attention to the man.

He cupped his mouth. "Okay, folks, we have six couples up here, ready to run the next race. One of them is our good friend, the sheriff. I'm not saying you should let him win, but if you beat him, you might want to watch your speedometer when you're driving through town."

Maddox waved at the crowd as they laughed.

"Is everyone ready?" the man asked.

We all nodded, and someone whistled. "Let's do this."

The man smiled. "All right. On your mark…"

"Good luck, Maddox," Addison shouted as we both turned to look at the guys.

She put her arms around me and pushed her chest into mine. I showed off my sexiest smile and rubbed my chest against hers.

"Get set…"

Maddox's mouth dropped open, and Tommy's eyes rounded to the size of the moon.

Addison blew a kiss, and I gave a finger wave despite the fact that I probably looked like I was trying way too hard.

"Go!"

"Middle, outside, middle, outside," Addison and I chanted as we took off to the finish line. We continued calling out our legs until we reached it.

I felt like we'd had good speed, but we had more walked than run.

"Olivia, look."

Addison and I almost fell as we turned around to face the direction we had come, only to see Tommy and Maddox crossing the finish line.

"Holy shit, we did it," I said.

Addison threaded her fingers with mine, and we jumped up and down. "It worked."

I laughed with joy. I couldn't believe we had actually beaten two Navy SEALs.

When we were finished celebrating, we untied our legs

and straightened our clothes. A man who looked vaguely familiar came over and handed Addison her shirt that she'd thrown in the grass.

"That was great, Addison."

"Thanks, Pete." She took her shirt and pulled it over her head. "Olivia, do you remember Pete from my wedding?"

That was where I recognized him from. "Hello. How are you?" I said to be polite.

"I'm great." He held up his phone. "I recorded the whole thing. You should have seen the guys' faces."

"Send me a copy?"

"I would love to." Pete looked up and over our shoulders. "Uh-oh. I'd better go. Congrats on winning," he said and took off.

Addison and I schooled our faces and turned around.

"You dirty cheat," Maddox said, putting his hands on his hips.

"Why, Maddox, whatever do you mean?" Addison said innocently.

He leaned down to her. "If we weren't in a school field full of people, I'd take you over my knee right now and spank you."

She bit her bottom lip. "Promise?"

"Woman, I'm this close to choking you."

"As long as your penis is inside me, you can choke me all you want."

Maddox threw up his hands and walked away.

Addison laughed. "Whoops. I think I made him mad." She ran after her husband. "Maddox, wait."

He stopped, and when Addison approached, he put his arm around her.

I let out the breath I'd been holding. "I was worried he was really angry with her."

"Don't tell her, but he was actually proud of you two for thinking on your feet like that. But that was after he got over his bruised ego."

"What do you think?" I asked him.

Tommy grinned. "I thought it was sneaky. But clever. It sure made it difficult for the two of us to walk to the finish line with hard-ons."

I put my hand in front of my mouth to cover my smile that refused to stay hidden. "I honestly didn't think it would work."

"You two were all but making out. Obviously, it worked."

"We weren't even close to making out."

He put his finger over my lips. "Shh…don't ruin it for me."

I pushed his hand away. "Addison's right. Men are controlled by their dicks."

"Duh."

I chuckled. "It's really hard to insult you when you agree with everything I say."

He put his arm around me and guided us toward Addison and Maddox. "Now, why would you want to insult me?"

I smiled. "I didn't say I *wanted* to. I just thought it was something that needed to be done since I won and you lost."

When we reached our friends, they had their arms around each other, and Addison was resting her chin on Maddox's chest.

She turned our way and laid her head over his heart. "Maddox was just telling me that he can't wait to paint our nails."

He snorted. "Yeah, something like that."

Addison laughed. "This is going to be so much fun." She looked up at her husband again. "I promise it won't kill you. I'll even let you pick out the color."

"Oh, really?" he asked sarcastically. "Did you hear that, Tommy? We get to pick out the color."

Tommy laughed. "I personally can't wait. After Olivia sees how good I am, she'll never ask me to do it for her again."

"Don't you mean, I *will* ask you to do it again?"

He held up the big, meaty hand that wasn't around me. "Not with these things." He leaned close to my ear. "They might be excellent at getting you off"—he straightened and finished the rest of his sentence, so everyone could hear— "but they are going to be shit when it comes to your nails."

I still couldn't wait to see how he'd do.

33

TOMMY

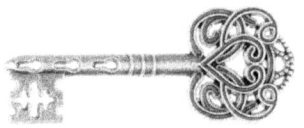

"*A*re you ready for some flag football?" Maddox asked me. "Is the knee going to be okay?"

I frowned. He was asking a legit question, but I didn't like being viewed as weak. "Not a problem."

He slapped his hand on my shoulder. "Good."

We headed over to the field where the game was going to take place. Olivia and Addison were already waiting there for us.

"Hey, ladies," I said.

Olivia smiled when she saw me, her face lighting up, and I couldn't help but grin back. I was feeling pretty fucking special.

"Addison told me about Maddox playing in high school. What about you?" she asked me.

"Sure did. I played pretty much every sport I could, growing up." And even though I'd made varsity my senior year, I was never going to get a scholarship or an NFL contract, which was why I'd set my sights on the military. "What about you?" I asked.

She laughed as if I'd told the best joke in the world. "My mom tried to put me in dance class when I was little. I have two left feet. After that, I think my parents knew not to push me toward anything that required any kind of coordination."

"I think you're plenty coordinated."

She blushed. "Tommy."

I laughed and leaned closer. "That wasn't a sexual innuendo, Liv. I was just stating a fact. When you walk, you're all graceful and shit. Hasn't anyone ever told you that?"

Her cheeks got redder. "No."

"Too bad." Because it was the truth. I didn't know if it was because she was confident or what, but she moved through the world like she was on a runway or a red carpet. It was sexy as hell. "Also, you and Addison just beat Maddox and me in a three-legged race. That takes coordination."

"I guess you're right."

I kissed her temple and stood up straight, losing my smile at the sight before me. "You've got to be shitting me."

"What?"

When I didn't respond, Olivia stood on her tiptoes. "What?"

I stepped behind her and picked her up just enough for her to see what I was seeing.

"What in the world?" she said.

I set her down, and by this time, Maddox and Addison were wondering what we were looking at.

"See those two? They're like an STD that won't go away. Annoying as fuck and always showing up when you think you're in the clear."

Olivia snorted.

"Who are they?" Maddox asked.

"Remember I told you about the troublemakers at the airport?"

Maddox chuckled. "You're kidding."

"Nope. That's Tweedledee and Tweedledum. What the fuck are they doing all the way out here?"

Frank shifted in our direction, and I ducked behind Maddox.

"Fuck. I hope he didn't see us. The last thing we need is trouble from them." I looked at Olivia. "Or Olivia getting into a fight with them."

She put her hands on her hips. "He called his sister a whore and me a bitch. I had every right to be mad."

I squeezed her side. "You sure did, sweetheart, but this guy is never going to change who he is. It's a lost cause, trying to argue with him." I stood and looked for Frank and Franny.

"They walked away," Addison said.

"Oh, thank God."

"Personally, I'd love to watch Olivia take him down," she said with a glint in her eye.

"See? Someone appreciates me," Olivia said.

"I appreciate you plenty. I just don't think Maddox would appreciate having to break up a fight and hauling your ass to jail."

"It's all good, Liv; I'd get you out," Addison said.

"Don't encourage her," Maddox said. "Tommy's right. There are plenty of people who still don't like me around here. And you know how rumors fly."

Addison put her hand on her husband's arm. "My poor baby."

Maddox scowled.

"But Maddox is right," she said. "When the former

sheriff resigned and left town, there were rumors that he was killed by the mob and that he ran away to elope. Neither of which is true."

"Don't worry, Maddox; I won't get in a fight. I know those two aren't worth it," Olivia told him.

"Attention, everyone," a man with a bullhorn said from the middle of the football field. "It's time for the annual flag football game."

The crowd cheered and laughed.

"Since this game is free and we don't make any money off it, I'm going to let you all pick your teams. You can start gathering on each side of me in a minute. But try to keep the numbers fair. If one side is larger than the other, I'll move some of you over. But until then, I think you are mature enough to handle it."

I held my fist out to Maddox. "I think we can win, no matter who is on our team."

He bumped my fist as Olivia snickered.

"What's so funny?"

"You thought you two were going to win last time, and…"

I grinned. "But this time, you're going to be cheering me on. Right?"

"I suppose." She smiled back at me.

"Well, well, well, what do we have here?"

I groaned, and the four of us turned to see Frank and Franny standing only a few feet away.

I'd gotten too comfortable these last few months of being a civilian. *Always check your six.*

Since Olivia promised no fighting, I nodded. "Hello." I was going to keep this short and civil.

"Shit, there's two of you," Frank said, looking at Maddox.

I raised an eyebrow. Sure, we were both tall and muscular, but that was where the similarities ended. Maddox was blond with green eyes. I was dark-haired with brown eyes. But I supposed to Frank's not-even-six feet—if I guessed correctly—we did stand out to him.

"What are you two doing here?" Franny asked.

"Visiting friends," I said.

"Yeah? We're visiting our cousins. You know the Donaldsons?" Frank asked.

I looked over at Addison, who was shaking her head ever so slightly in a way that told me the Donaldsons were bad news. "Can't say that I do."

"All right, folks, it's time to pick your teams."

Thank God for small favors.

"Sorry to cut the conversation short, but we gotta go and play."

As Maddox and I headed over to one side of the field, I heard Franny tell her brother, "Go play against them."

"Good idea, sis."

I looked at Maddox and rolled my eyes. Flag football or not, Frank was going to get his ass handed to him.

A couple of other guys followed Frank, and Maddox leaned over to me. "Those are the two Donaldson boys. They don't know how to stay out of trouble. My deputies are always picking them up for something. Usually minor and always misdemeanors, but it's like they can't *not* break the law. If Frank is anything like his cousins, I can see why he picked a fight with you at the airport."

I shook my head. "Must be a family thing."

The announcer lifted the bullhorn in the air. "Since this is a make-no-money game, we also don't have uniforms. If you're new here, we do shirts versus skins. This is your chance to vote which team is which, folks."

I leaned over to Maddox. "I suddenly feel like a piece of meat."

He chuckled.

Bullhorn pointed to the opposite team. "Everyone in favor of this team being skins?"

There was a good amount of cheering.

Bullhorn waved his hands in a manner that signaled for everyone to be quiet. He pointed to our team. "Now, everyone in favor of this side being skins?"

The cheering before was nothing compared to what it was this time. Addison put her fingers between her lips and whistled.

"Your wife is trouble," I said in Maddox's ear.

He grinned. "Don't I know it." He nodded toward his wife. "Olivia's not much better."

I followed his gaze to see her cupping her hands, and she whooped to the crowd.

"This team it is. Take off your shirts, fellas." He eyed the two women on our team. "Ladies, you are free to leave your shirts on. Just don't forget they're your teammates, men."

"We got it," one of the women yelled.

They stripped off their shirts to show they had sports bras underneath.

"Smart," I said.

"They play every year and come prepared," Maddox said. "We're lucky to have them," he said loudly enough for our whole team to hear.

"Thanks, Maddox," the woman said. "Now, strip."

Maddox and I laughed as we yanked off our tees and threw them at Olivia and Addison.

"Let's kick some ass," I said.

———

About an hour later, we did just that. I watched Frank walk off the field with his head down. I hoped that it was finally the last time I saw him and his sister.

34

OLIVIA

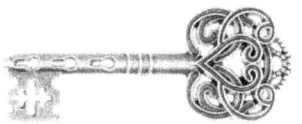

J sighed with contentment when baby Thane fell asleep on my chest as I lay on Addison's couch, watching a Disney movie. It almost made me want to have one of my own. Addison and Spencer were cuddled up on the recliner, and I had a wistful feeling I was missing something in my life. I had always thought I was married to my job and wouldn't have time for a family. I'd had no idea I was harboring a secret longing for maybe having one of my own someday.

It was my last night in Brook Creek, and I was feeling a little melancholy. That was probably where these unusual thoughts were stemming from. I was going to miss hanging out with Addison and Maddox. And I was really going to miss being around Tommy.

I'd heard from the police that morning. There were no fingerprints besides Tommy's, Derek's, and mine, and they were still collecting results from DNA on the letters and envelopes, particularly the seal.

But even though we didn't know who had sent me the

letters, there hadn't been any more, and I didn't feel right about pulling Tommy away from his vacation.

I was only going to be an hour away, and I was already working on ways I could come and visit. I just worried that I would look too desperate. Tommy had never mentioned seeing each other beyond this trip. Then again, neither had I. But Virginia was a long way away from Iowa. I couldn't even make relationships work when I lived in the same town as the person I was dating. How could I possibly do it from half a country away?

"Hopefully, after the movie, we can put the boys to bed and watch a grown-up one," Addison said to me. "If it's not too late. I know you have to drive back tomorrow."

"No, I'd like that."

"Did you want me to put Thane to bed now?"

I rubbed the little guy's back. "No, I'm good. It's my last night to get baby snuggles, so I might as well take advantage of it."

Addison smiled. "I never took you for a baby snuggler."

I chuckled. "Me neither. But he's pretty hard to resist."

I heard the sound of heavy footsteps coming up from the basement. Tommy had gone down there with Maddox after dinner to go over some plans on what he wanted to do to finish up the lower level.

The two men stopped in the kitchen and were speaking in low voices to each other.

"What do you think is going on in there?" I asked.

She arched her back, sticking her ear out since she was closer to the kitchen than I was. She relaxed and shook her head. "No idea. I can't hear what they're saying."

The two men rounded the corner, and my mouth dropped open when I saw them first.

Addison spun around in her chair, holding on to Spencer so he wouldn't fall. "What is going on?"

Tommy and Maddox were wearing jeans, no shirts, and bow ties.

Tommy held up a bottle of nail polish. "We came to pay up. And we're not quite naked butlers, but we thought this was pretty close."

Maddox sat down at Addison's feet.

"Whose idea was this?" she asked.

"I kind of forgot about the bet," I said.

"I told you," Maddox said to Tommy. "We can always leave," he said with a smile to his wife.

"Oh, don't you dare."

He chuckled and picked up a foot. "I figured as much."

"Daddy, what you doing?" Spencer asked as Tommy sat down by my feet and faced me.

"I'm going to paint Mommy's toenails."

Spencer held up a little foot. "Me, too."

"After Mommy, buddy. You have to wait your turn."

I had to admit, I was shocked that such an alpha male would be okay with painting his son's toenails. Some guys would shut down the idea.

"Don't you dare," Addison said to Maddox. "There is no way he'll sit still long enough for it to dry, and we'll have streaks of nail polish all over the house."

Maddox winced. "Sorry, buddy. Mommy makes a good point. Maybe when you're a little older."

"Now."

Addison picked up Spencer's foot and blew a raspberry on it. The sweet boy giggled and seemed to forget all about getting his nails painted.

"So, what color did you pick out for me?" I asked Tommy. "Some sort of red?"

He grinned. "Fuck-me red," he said, whispering the word *fuck* so Spencer couldn't hear.

I wiggled my toes. "Have at it."

He picked up a foot and massaged the ball of it. "At this time, I would like to remind you that I suck at this. But I give great foot massages, if you'd like to change your order from nail painting to foot massages."

His hands really did feel great, but I wanted to see this big manly man do my nails more than I wanted a rubdown.

I smiled and shook my head. "No dice."

He shrugged. "Can't blame a guy for trying." He unscrewed the bottle, set it on the coffee table, and pulled out the brush. He painted my big toe and pulled my foot back to inspect his handiwork. "Not too bad."

I lifted my leg and looked. "Good job, stud. Let's see you do the little ones now," I teased.

He pulled my foot back and went to work on my other four toes.

His brow furrowed in concentration as he painted. He was adorable.

Even though he had warned me that he was going to be bad at this job, he was still trying his best for me.

Thane stirred on my chest, and I suddenly wondered what it would be like to have Tommy paint my nails while I lay on our couch and held our baby as he slept on me.

I closed my eyes and tried to shake the image as my heart began to pound.

It was one thing to want a family someday. It was another to want it with my vacation fling.

I had never even pictured having kids with my past boyfriends.

Holy shit. I was in deep with this guy.

"Olivia. Olivia."

I opened my eyes.

Tommy smiled. "I'm done." He tilted his head. "Are you okay?"

"Yeah. I was drifting off there; I was so relaxed."

"Sorry."

"Do not apologize. That felt amazing."

"You want to take a look at my work?"

I lifted one foot and then the other. There was a good amount of paint on my skin where it met my nail in a few places, but I didn't mind.

"I love it," I said with sincerity. "Thank you."

Tommy twisted the cap back on the bottle. "You're welcome."

"Want to help me put this little guy to bed?"

"You don't have to do that," Addison said. "Maddox is almost done."

Tommy stood and carefully lifted the sleeping baby from my chest. "You two fed us dinner. The least we can do is help you out."

"I appreciate it," Addison said.

"Me, too," Maddox added from the floor. He looked at his older son. "One down, one to go. Right, Spence?"

Spencer laughed.

Tommy carried Thane to his room while I followed.

"Put him on the changing table," I said as I started opening up the dresser drawers. I found what I needed in the second from the top. I selected a pair of pajamas with bears on them and carried them over to Thane and Tommy.

Tommy already had Thane undressed and was changing his diaper. "Can you believe he's sleeping through all of this?"

"No," I said as a lump filled my throat. Again, I was bombarded with thoughts of Tommy and me together, getting our baby ready for bed. Instead of a little blond-haired boy, ours would have a head of dark locks.

"Olivia."

I met Tommy's face. "Hmm?"

He held out his hand. "PJs?"

"Oh, right."

Tommy dressed Thane and then slowly lowered him into his crib.

We both held our breath to make sure the baby didn't wake up.

After a good minute, Tommy turned to me and put his hands on my upper arms. "Are you sure you're okay?"

35

TOMMY

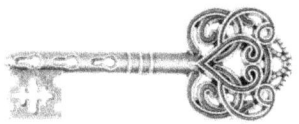

Something seemed to be weighing on Olivia's mind, but rather than talking about it, she threw herself in my arms and kissed me.

I tried to fight it at first because I didn't want her to feel like she couldn't talk to me, but when she started rubbing herself over my groin, my body soon won the battle with my brain.

"We shouldn't be doing this here," I said, eyeing the sleeping baby a few feet away. "Let's go back to my place."

Olivia cupped my length. "Or we could go into the bathroom." She squeezed.

"Okay, let's go into the bathroom."

Man, I was super easy.

We peeked out into the hall and then snuck across it to the bathroom. As soon as the door was closed, she kissed me again.

"We have to make this quick before we get caught," I said as I pulled my shirt over my head.

"I know," she said, pushing my jeans off my hips far enough so that she could grab on to my dick.

I shuddered and looked down at her clothes. Olivia often wore skirts and dresses, but today wasn't one of those days, which was a shame. I could have set her on the counter, lifted up her hem, and slipped inside her.

We were going to have to go with plan B.

I twirled her around and pushed against her back. "Bend over the counter."

She did as I'd asked and rubbed her ass against me to let me know she was ready.

I pushed her shorts and underwear down to her knees and spread her legs just enough. Pushing a finger inside her, I groaned. She was soaked.

I rubbed against her G-spot for a few seconds before I replaced my digit with my cock.

"Ready?"

"Yes."

I thrust inside her with one smooth move, and I had to bite my cheek to keep from groaning at how good she felt.

I wrapped my arms around her body, touching her everywhere as I began to thrust. I pushed my hands under her bra and squeezed her breasts, and I pulled her back against me over and over.

Little sounds were beginning to escape her mouth. I was half-worried Maddox and Addison would hear and half-worried we'd wake up the baby.

I pulled a hand from under her shirt and glided it up. I was aiming for her mouth, but when I reached her throat, something told me to stop. When I cupped her there, her pussy tightened around my dick.

When she made another noise, I put pressure on her. "Shh…you gotta be quiet."

She nodded and clapped one of her hands over her mouth.

"Do you want me to stop?"

She shook her head.

"Do you remember our safe word?"

She nodded.

"Good."

I tightened my hold a little as I slammed into her. I didn't know how much longer I could hold off my orgasm, but I needed to make sure Olivia came first.

I went to pull my hand from her throat to move it to her clit, but she slammed one hand against mine.

I grinned. Who knew that hard-ass Olivia Mayer liked to be choked?

Me. I did.

I gently squeezed her throat, and she started contracting around me.

"Yes, Olivia, come," I whispered.

She shook in my arms, her hands falling down to the counter to catch herself before she fell.

She pushed her ass into me, and I came with a hot rush.

We stood there, gasping for air, with our shorts and pants around our knees and my forehead resting on her back.

I really hated that she was leaving tomorrow because I wanted to explore her sexuality so much more. So much had changed in a week, and I couldn't imagine what I might find out if we had a month together.

I heard movement down the hall in the living room and knew it was time for us to get dressed.

I reluctantly left her body and pulled up her shorts. I tried to button them for her, but she brushed my hand away.

"I got it."

I tugged up my own pants and fastened them. "You okay?" Maybe I had taken things too far with the choking. "I didn't hurt you, did I?"

She lifted her head, her eyes filled with shock. "No."

"Whew. You had me worried there for a second."

She arranged her bra and shirt back into place while I picked up my own tee from the floor and put it on.

She threw her arms around my neck. "You didn't hurt me. That was great."

"Then, what's wrong?"

She opened her mouth, but I stopped her.

"And don't tell me nothing."

She smiled. "I'm going to miss you."

"Ah, shit. I'm going to miss you, too." It was on the tip of my tongue to tell her to invite me back to Des Moines with her, but I didn't. If she wanted me to come, she would think of asking me on her own. "I know tomorrow will be here shortly, but you and I still have tonight. What do you say we get out of here?"

"But I told Addison we would watch a movie."

I was disappointed, but it was her last night with Addison, too. "I understand."

She studied my face. "Screw it. Addison lives a lot closer than you. Let's go back to your place."

I grinned. "Yay for winning."

She laughed. "Now, I just have to go break the news to my friend." She stepped away and opened the door.

I grabbed her wrist. "If you really want to stay, please don't leave because I pressured you."

She smiled. "I'm not. I really want to go back with you."

I sighed with relief. Our time wasn't over yet.

But it was coming to an end all too soon.

36

OLIVIA

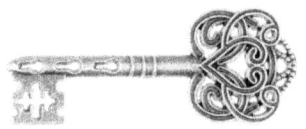

*I*t was going-home day. A week ago, I'd thought my vacation was going to drag out and last forever. But time had flown.

I stood in Addison and Maddox's driveway, hugging Addison good-bye.

"Come back again, okay?" she said to me. "Don't make it another few years either."

I squeezed. "I will. I promise." Especially if I knew Tommy was going to be in town.

I stepped back and gave Maddox, Thane, and Spencer hugs. And then it was Tommy's turn.

He pulled me into a bear hug and buried my face in his chest. I was really afraid that I was going to cry right there for everyone to see.

I looked up into his face and forced a smile. "I'm going to miss you, you big oaf."

"Ooh." He pretended to be hurt. "I'm going to miss you, too, you little pixie."

A genuine laugh came out of me. "I guess this is it." I had no reason left to stay.

"Maybe the three of us can come and visit you this weekend," Addison offered.

I immediately brightened at the idea until I saw the guys exchange looks.

"Uh, Addy, we were planning to get a lot of work done on the basement this weekend."

"Oh crap. That's right." She shrugged. "Maybe just me then."

"I'd like that." Not as much, but that was neither here nor there.

I climbed behind my wheel and forced myself to start my car. The longer I hesitated to leave, the more everyone was going to think something was wrong.

I rolled down the window and waved as I pulled out of the driveway and onto the street.

"Call if you need anything," Tommy yelled.

"I will."

"He's serious, Olivia. You'd better call us," Addison said.

I smiled. "I will." I put an X across my chest. "Promise."

With one more wave, I put my vehicle in gear and drove away. By the time I reached the highway, I was wiping away more tears than I was comfortable with admitting.

———

I needed to keep my brain occupied before I got too sad about missing Tommy, so I went straight to work. Derek knew I was coming and had an afternoon coffee waiting for me.

"You're the best assistant," I said as I pushed open my office door.

"Says the woman who was planning to fire me less than a week ago."

"I'm allowed to change my mind." I flipped through the messages he'd handed me.

Most of them were potential clients who wanted to hire me. I was going to have to wade through them and decide who I wanted to meet with and who was going to be an outright no. There were simply too many of them and only one of me.

But we had a couple of associates that I could kick some of the cases down to. Even the first and second years were good because we didn't hire bad attorneys. Or at least, we tried not to. We'd had to fire a couple over the years.

"Can you ask Bridget to come in here? I have a couple of things I need her to look into, so I can get started on Tate's lawsuit case."

Bridget was our investigator and one of the best there was. We were lucky to have her at our firm.

Derek looked uncomfortable. "About that."

"Already something bad? I just got here. There aren't any more letters that you haven't told me about, are there?"

If Tommy or even Addison had told Derek to leave me alone on vacation, I was going to be pissed. Yes, I'd had a great time, but if something had been kept from me, there was going to be hell to pay. I was not a child.

"First things first." Derek shook his head and handed me a pile of mail that was in his other hand.

"Junk mail, junk mail, a wedding invitation, junk mail, a reminder to schedule my six-month checkup at the dentist, junk mail, junk mail, and more junk mail."

He pulled one last message slip out from his pocket. "Also, your mom called."

I sighed. "What does she want?"

"To know if you're going to your cousin's wedding next month. She wanted you to know that she'll be going a few days early, so you can't ride together."

My father had been the glue that held our little family together, but he'd died from a heart condition when I was in high school. It was the same heart condition that had been discovered after I was adopted but before my parents had tried to adopt a second child. That was the main reason they had been unable to adopt another child. So, now, it was just my mom and me, and we weren't close. We were nothing alike, and I always got the impression that my father was the one who had wanted children while my mom had done it to make him happy. It was never said to me, but she always lacked a certain warmth. Not just to me. It was her personality. How my joyful, full-of-life father had ever married her was something I'd never understand.

"Joke's on her. I'm not going to the wedding."

Derek's mouth opened in surprise. "Did you not get invited?"

"Oh, I did. But Cynthia has always been a bitch. Trust me, we'll both be happier when I don't show up." I pulled up my chair and sat down. "Now, will you tell Bridget to come to my office, please?"

"Bridget's been told that you have to handle investigating this case on your own."

"Excuse me?"

"The other partners decided that since you are doing another case pro bono, they can't afford to have Bridget do more work when you're not bringing in any billable hours. They really need her working on the Schultz Auto case."

"Damn it." Schultz Auto Sales was a big client who paid our firm a lot of money. I understood that it took top priority. "I knew we should have hired another investigator."

"You tried, remember? You didn't like any of them."

"Right now, a bad one would be better than no one." This was really going to cut into my time on other cases.

"Do you still want me to get her?"

"No." I was just going to handle it myself.

———

By the time Friday evening rolled around, I was exhausted. Despite being busy, I still missed Tommy. Unfortunately, I hadn't had a minute to spare to talk to him on the phone, and I'd barely texted with him.

It was a good reminder that relationships didn't work for me.

When I got home that night, I was on alert as I entered my house, but as usual, nothing was wrong. I hadn't received any more threats in the mail either. I didn't quite think everything would be back to normal until Tate's case was over, but I hoped the mail that had been delivered to my home was the peak of terrorization I received from the mysterious person. And I was still optimistic that there would be a DNA match sooner rather than later.

I quickly grabbed a yogurt and banana from the kitchen and went to my room. I stuffed food down my throat as I got ready for bed. These days, I was all about multitasking.

When I was finished, I threw the container and peel in

the garbage and headed to bed for another lonely night of sleep.

Right before I crawled in, I ran my fingers over the book Tommy had left at my house. I should put it on my bookshelf, but for some reason, I couldn't bring myself to do that. Every once in a while, I looked to see what he was reading on Kindle, too. So far, he hadn't signed up for his own account, and it pleased me way too much.

Someday soon, I was going to have to push him out of my mind and forget about him because he clearly had a home and a life back in Virginia, and he had never indicated he wanted anything more than hot vacation sex.

Today wasn't going to be that day.

———

The next morning, all thoughts of exorcising Tommy from my mind were gone when I stepped outside.

37

TOMMY

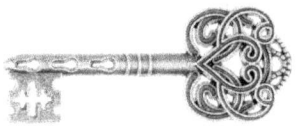

J had just finished hauling in a load of drywall to Maddox's basement when my phone rang.

It was still early in the morning. The weather had been very humid lately, so Maddox and I had been getting up at dawn to start work before we felt like we were being suffocated from the heat.

Whoever was calling me at this hour was either an early bird or they were calling about something important.

Turned out to be both.

I was surprised to see Olivia's name on my caller ID. We'd barely exchanged any messages all week, which let me know just how she felt about me. It was apparent that I felt more for her than she did me.

"Hello?"

"Hey, Tommy." She sounded hesitant, as if I wouldn't want to hear from her.

"Hey yourself."

"Are you busy?"

"Um"—I looked at Maddox—"just working on the basement, but we were about to take a break."

He nodded and went upstairs.

"Is there something I can help you with?"

Jesus, we'd gone from spending every night together to
some weird formality. As if I hadn't made her come multiple
times.

"I'm not sure. I have a situation, and I guess I was
looking for your input."

My chest puffed out. Of all people, she had come to me
with her problem.

"I'll do my best. Hit me."

"When I woke up this morning, there was a dead cat on
my doorstep. Do you think I should be worried?"

"I'll be there in forty-five minutes."

"But I live at least an hour away."

"Not with the way I'll be driving."

"You don't have to come, Tommy. I called you for advice."

"Olivia, we're not going to argue about this. I'm coming."

"I don't think it's that big of a—"

"Call the police. I'll see you in forty-five." I hung up the
phone and took the stairs two at a time.

———

Maddox gave me the keys to his SUV without hesitation,
and I took off for Olivia's after stopping to pick up my bag. I
wasn't planning to come back to Brook Creek anytime soon.

Because of the small detour to grab my stuff, it took me
an hour to get to her place. When I arrived, I called her as I
pulled into her driveway.

"Open your garage door," I said after she answered.

I hopped out of Maddox's SUV and marched into the garage to see her standing in the doorway.

"Did the police show up yet?"

"No."

I cursed. I understood this wasn't an emergency situation and Olivia's life wasn't in immediate danger, but I was frustrated that they hadn't shown up yet.

I couldn't help but picture her dead on her doorstep instead of a cat.

"Come inside," she said. "I'll show you that poor animal."

We walked to the front door. When she opened it, I knelt down and studied it the best I could without stepping outside in case there was evidence I might disturb. It was the reason I had come in through the garage.

The first thing I noticed was the absence of blood. The second was the marks on the cat that suggested it had been hit by a car. Those two things made me feel slightly better, as whoever had brought the cat here had found an animal that was already dead instead of killing it on her front step. Or worse, torturing it.

Just as I stood, a police car pulled up in front of the house. The two officers who had come to Olivia's office last week stepped out of the car. It made sense that they would dispatch the same officers, and that might explain the delay in them showing up. Didn't make me feel any better about their late presence though.

"Next time, don't open the door," I told Olivia. "Someone could have placed the cat here in order to lure you outside, where they could attack you."

She snorted her laughter, and I shot her a look.

"I'm not joking, Olivia. You need to take your safety more seriously."

"I think you're overreacting."

"And I think you're underreacting."

The cops were reaching hearing distance.

"We'll discuss this later," I said, pausing any further arguments from her.

38

OLIVIA

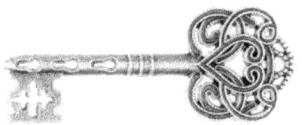

I didn't know where Tommy got off on ordering me around. This was my life, my house, and my profession being targeted.

But I bit my tongue to keep from saying any more until after the police left.

I could tell they were less than impressed with the *present* that had been dropped off on my doorstep. This made me feel both satisfied that I knew Tommy was overreacting yet simultaneously worried that if something did happen to me, the police wouldn't care.

At least they had taken the poor cat with them to the lab, and I wouldn't have to dispose of it myself.

I shut the door and faced Tommy. "Let me make one thing clear. You are not the boss of me."

He took a step back and frowned. "When did I ever say I was your boss?" He laughed. "I am very well aware that you are your own person. It's one of the things I find sexy as hell about you."

I crossed my arms over my chest. "You and I were fighting, and you decided when to cut the conversation short and that we would talk about it later." I really hated that he'd had the last word. "Maybe I wasn't done talking about it."

A truly confused look crossed his face, and I swore the corners of his mouth twitched. If he was laughing at me, I wasn't going to be held responsible for my actions.

It took several seconds for Tommy to speak. "Okay, first of all, we were having a *discussion*. We were not fighting. Secondly, I did not cut you off because I get to decide when and where we talk about things. I stopped the conversation because the officers were walking up to the front door. If we were fighting, as you put it, would you have really wanted them to hear us?"

I pursed my lips together because I didn't want to answer. "No," I reluctantly admitted.

"And when I said we would discuss it later, I was merely letting you know we could finish when we were alone again. That's all I meant."

Now, I felt like a fool for overreacting. Something I had just accused him of doing earlier. "Go ahead. Laugh."

He shook his head. "I wouldn't dare." He stepped forward. "I really would like to kiss you though."

"Then, what are you waiting for?"

Tommy hauled me into his arms, and I practically inhaled him when he put his lips on mine.

He carried me into the living room, and we fell onto the couch. His shirt went flying, and he attacked my pants. "I'm sorry, Liv. This is going to be a quick fuck. It's only been a few days, but I need to be inside you."

I had no complaints, and I went for his fly as soon as I was naked on the bottom.

Tommy's shaft sprang out into my hand, but I barely got

to touch it before he pushed my hands away and drove inside me.

I cried out in pleasure. *Oh, yes.*

If I had Tommy fucking me before bed every night, I had a feeling I would be a lot more ready to take on the day the next morning.

He lifted my ass and pounded into me. With every thrust, he dragged my clit over his pelvis, and it wasn't long before I was panting and begging for him to make me come.

Two more lunges forward, and we both exploded. I bucked my hips as he held on and poured his seed into me.

After we both collapsed, I could still feel him twitching inside me.

I pushed his hair off his sweaty forehead. "I needed that. It's been a long week."

"Did you put the cat there yourself, so you could finally have an excuse for me to come here?"

I smacked his arm. "Bad joke."

He smiled. "You're right." He kissed my chest over my breastbone even though we hadn't bothered to take off my shirt. "Is you being busy why I barely heard from you?"

I replayed the words in my head. Could there be a chance he'd missed me, or was he just asking out of curiosity?

"Yes. I've been working on Tate's case, plus helping a first-year associate with another. Our firm's investigator is pretty much working full-time on a big-name client that we can't afford to lose. She doesn't have much time to do anything else even though I know she'd help me if I needed her to."

"When is the big-name client's case going to court, so your investigator can help you?"

They weren't going to court. At least, not yet.

"They are starting negotiations next week. If things don't work out there, court would be next. It'll be a while. Court is always the last step because it costs the most money and time."

"Is that what's going to happen with Tate's case?"

"Maybe."

Tate and I were probably going to try to sit down with the Scotts and get them to dismiss the case, but I had a feeling we were going to have to threaten to countersue in order to do that. And knowing the Scotts, they probably weren't going to back down even though we had a good case. They had slandered Tate's name all over the media. If we went to court, I was going to make sure Tate saw a good amount of money. The poor kid deserved it.

Tommy lifted his eyes. "You can't say any more because of privilege, right?"

I smiled. "You got it."

"I get it."

"Thank you. Guys I've dated in the past didn't understand."

"Same for me. I usually couldn't even tell girlfriends where I was going when we got sent out of the country. Some people don't understand that a job requirement is to keep our lips sealed."

I'd never really thought about Tommy and me having things in common because his job had been so different from mine. It was a relief to not have someone press me for answers simply because they were curious.

And I was really glad I would never have to worry about Tommy being sent out of the country without me knowing where he was going.

I closed my eyes.

I was thinking about him in future terms way too much, and I needed to make it stop.

"You okay up there?" he asked.

"I'm fine." I pressed on his shoulders. "But we'd probably better get up. I have some work I have to do today."

That was just an excuse. I really didn't want to lie in his arms and think about how much I was going to miss him.

39

TOMMY

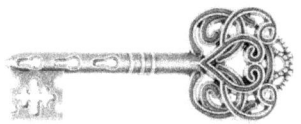

Sunday afternoon, I dropped Olivia off at work. She had insisted on going in to work on a few things, and I had insisted that I would be the one to take her. I worried about her being in her office building on the weekend, but she assured me many lawyers worked seven days a week and she wouldn't be alone.

That was reassuring information, but what made me feel even better was when I talked to the security guard near the entrance. I took him for former military and knew just how to make him a new friend of mine. By the time I left, he was more than happy to keep an extra eye out for any suspicious activity, especially regarding Olivia.

I headed back to her neighborhood and parked in her driveway. Then, I took out a notebook and began writing down house numbers. After that, I strode up to the front door of the house directly across the street and knocked firmly.

A woman who was old enough to be my grandmother answered.

I gave her my best golly-gee-whiz smile as she eyed me through the screen door.

I took off the baseball cap I had been wearing and said, "Afternoon, ma'am. I was wondering if I could talk to you real quick."

She looked down at my notebook and then back up at me. "I don't want to buy anything."

"Oh, no, ma'am, I'm not selling anything."

"Then, what are you here for?"

I pointed to Olivia's house. "Do you know the lady who lives there? She's my friend, and recently, someone has been causing her trouble. Did you happen to see any activity late Friday night or early Saturday morning?"

The woman shook her head. "I don't know her. She's rarely home. And I didn't see anything."

Before I could get another question out, the lady slammed the door in my face.

"Nice speaking with you, too." I crossed her house number off my list.

The next two neighbors to the right hadn't seen anything. Neither had the house two doors down from Olivia. Her next-door neighbor wasn't home. I walked to the other side of Olivia's home and knocked there, too.

I was feeling defeated when I knocked on the door on the other side of the grumpy, old biddy. I had successfully made a full circle without a single thing to show for it.

The door opened to a man about my age, but I no longer had the energy to give him a hundred-watt smile. My half-assed one was going to have to do.

"Can I help you?" he asked.

"I'm not selling anything," I said first. The old lady wasn't the only one who'd thought I was soliciting. "I just have a few questions for you, if that's okay."

"I can sure try. It depends on what you're asking."

I pointed to Olivia's house and asked him if he had seen anything the night before.

He shook his head. "Sorry. No."

"Thanks anyway," I said and turned on my heel to leave.

"But you're more than welcome to check my security cameras."

———

The neighbor, Troy, not only had a camera pointed at Olivia's house, but he'd also caught the whole incident. The best part was that it was all uploaded to the cloud. All he had to do was send me the link.

The image showed an individual in black, carrying a bag to Olivia's front door and dumping it out. They were covered from head to toe, so I couldn't see any identifying features, but from the person's height, build, and walk, I'd bet my left nut it was a woman.

The frustrating part was that the car was parked on the street. From the angle, there was no way to get a full license plate. It was an Iowa plate that started with a six. But I did know it was a dark Mercedes.

I hopped in my car, ready to show the evidence to Olivia to see if she recognized anything and then send it on to the police. I left the neighborhood, following the same direction the car had pulled away from her place, and I wasn't far when I noticed a cluster of businesses. A bank, some restaurants, a few other miscellaneous stores.

I made a quick right turn and headed into the parking

lot. I really wanted to check the bank's surveillance cameras because banks always had the highest security, but it was Sunday, and they were closed.

Unless...

The bank was part of a large chain, and those big banks often had twenty-four-hour customer service. Figuring I had nothing to lose, I pulled out my phone and Googled for phone numbers. I found one immediately and hit dial.

A woman answered with the name of the bank and a cheerful tone. "My name is Marci. How can I help you today?"

"This is an odd request and one you're probably going to have to forward to your supervisor. I'm looking into seeing if I can access a local branch's security cameras. I realize that today is Sunday, but banks often have security guards do patrol. Is there any way I can speak to them and potentially have them give me access?"

"I'm sorry. What did you say your name was, and who do you work for?"

"Sorry, miss. My name is...Tom, and I work for"—*shit*. I couldn't lie and say I was a police officer, but I quickly remembered what Olivia had told me the day before about having to do all the legwork because their investigator was tied up on other cases—"a law firm actually." And I gave them Olivia's firm's name.

I crossed my fingers that if anyone called her work, she would answer since it was a weekend and vouch for me.

"Let me see what I can do. Hold, please."

"Thank you."

40

OLIVIA

I looked up from my computer to see Tommy walk into my office. I checked the clock on the corner of my screen. "You're early."

"I need you to see something." His demeanor was serious, so I knew something was up.

"Okay," I said, pulling my laptop closed.

"Leave that open."

I lifted the lid back up.

"Do you mind if I sit?"

"Give me a second." I closed down anything that had privileged information on it. "What's going on?" I asked as I stood.

He slipped into my chair, which was pretty impressive for someone his size. He'd told me that I was graceful, but I thought he was. Although I would never use that word to describe him to his face.

"You'll see in a second." He plugged his phone into my computer. He pressed a few folders and opened a video.

It was black and white and taken at night.

I leaned forward. "Is that my house?"

"Yes."

I watched a car pull up and someone get out. They grabbed a plastic garbage bag from the trunk. "Is the dead cat in there?" I asked. "How did you get this?"

"Your neighbor. He was very nice and let me scan through his security footage." He pointed to the screen. "Do you recognize the person? Or the car?"

I studied the video, but the person, who did appear to be female, was covered in black from head to toe, except for their face. But she never lifted her head enough to be fully caught on the camera. "It looks like a white woman, but that's all I've got."

"Same here," he said.

As for the car, it was a dark four-door sedan. "I don't know about the vehicle either. I'm really bad at identifying cars."

"It's a Mercedes."

"I'm sorry, but that's not much help."

One of my partners drove a Mercedes, but I really didn't think he was the one threatening me. Especially since he was a man and this appeared to be a woman on the screen.

Tommy ended the video and pulled up another one. This one was from a different location.

"Where's this?"

"It's the street in front of the bank by your house. I figured since it was the direction the woman drove away, there was a chance she was caught on other cameras, too."

"But it's Sunday."

He grinned at me. "I called them, told them I was an investigator for your firm, and they were happy to help."

My jaw dropped. "You're a genius."

He laughed.

"I'm serious. That was very smart of you."

"Thanks. Now, focus on the windshield."

I watched as the car drove past the bank. "It's too fast."

"Let me slow it down for you."

Tommy played the video in slow-motion. While the bank had better cameras than my neighbor, it was hard to see.

"Once more, please."

"You got it."

I leaned back and then into the screen again. "It almost looks like…"

"Who?"

"This is going to sound crazy."

"Just tell me."

"It looks like Miranda Scott, Annabelle's mom, but…"

"But what?"

I had to think of how to put it into words. "She's…so high-class. Like, the times I've seen her outside court, she never drives. She always has a driver. She won't even touch the door handle to let herself in. But she picked up roadkill off the side of the highway? It just doesn't fit."

"Desperate people do desperate things when they feel like they're backed into a corner."

I shook my head. "But she doesn't even acknowledge my existence. Her husband has made it clear he hates me. Miranda Scott acts like I don't even exist."

"It doesn't mean she doesn't know about you."

I supposed he was right, but…

"I can't say for certain that it's her when I'm not positive. That would make me no better than the Scotts—accusing someone of a crime without evidence."

Tommy put his arm around my waist, pulling me close to him, and smiled.

"Why do you look so happy?"

"I have a license plate number."

I gasped. I had been looking so closely at the driver that I didn't think to look at the plate. "Why didn't you just say that?"

"I wanted to know what you thought first. Besides, who knows when the police will question her? If there was a chance you knew the person, I thought it was best to keep an eye out."

I lifted a shoulder. "I guess."

"What do you need to do to finish up here? Because I was thinking we'd take a little trip to the police station."

41

TOMMY

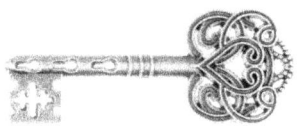

*I*t had been two days since Olivia and I had taken my findings to the police. They hadn't been impressed with the two of us showing up at first, but after I'd explained what I had found, their mood had changed.

Now, if I could just get them to call us back with an update so I knew Olivia was safe, I could relax a little. I could tell she was getting antsy, too.

She'd practically begged me to let her drive herself to work that morning. The only reason I had said yes was because someone needed to be in the house when the security company showed up to install her cameras.

I'd made her promise to call me when she arrived at the office and again when she was leaving work. She had actually complied with both calls.

I looked at my watch.

Her last call had been forty-five minutes ago, and she wasn't home yet. She lived less than thirty minutes from work. And when I'd called her a minute ago, she hadn't answered the phone.

I began to pace back and forth.

The installation guy turned around to look at me.

I held up my hands. "Sorry. I'm just a little anxious."

"I'm almost finished here, and then hopefully, you won't have to be anxious anymore."

"Yeah." *Right.*

I was always going to worry about Olivia.

Always? Wow. I hadn't seen that one coming.

My phone rang, and I answered it without even looking at the caller ID. "Where are you?" I demanded.

"Sitting on my deck, drinking a beer. Is there a crime in that?"

"Maddox." I ran my hand down my face and stepped outside, so I could pace out there. "No. I thought you were Olivia. She left work almost fifty minutes ago. She's not home yet, and she didn't answer when I called her."

"Still nothing back from the police?"

"No. They're worthless." I cringed. "I'm sorry, Mad Dog. I didn't mean that. I'm just…"

"Scared about the woman you love."

I stopped walking and replayed Maddox's sentence in my head. "What?"

He laughed. "Come on, dude. Don't act like you didn't know."

"No, I…I don't—"

Maddox's laughter died. "Oh, you didn't know. I thought it was obvious that you'd developed feelings for her."

"Developed feelings, yes. But that doesn't mean I'm in love."

"Think about it. You spent a whole week with her. She slept in your bed every night. She called you for advice about a possibly dangerous situation, and you split so fast that you left a dust cloud behind you. Now, you're probably wearing a hole in the carpet because you can't sit still from worrying. And she's not even a half hour late."

I swallowed. "I don't necessarily know that that's love."

"Would you worry about me if I were twenty minutes later than expected?"

"No, because you can take care of yourself."

"And Olivia can't? Sure, she's a female, which makes her smaller, but she's pretty feisty. And didn't you tell me you'd armed her with pepper spray and a self-defense key chain?"

"Yeah, but—"

"Yeah, but nothing. How would you feel right now if something happened to her?"

A sense of doom settled over me at the thought of her being hurt—or worse, killed. I didn't want to think about a world without Olivia Mayer in it.

As if a lightbulb went off over my head, I realized the enormity of my thoughts.

I sighed. "Fuck me."

Maddox burst out laughing. "Man, I wish I could see your face right now."

"I'm sure it looks like I'm in deep shit."

"Hey, you'll figure it out."

"Yeah, you say that. But Olivia has never once expressed wanting anything more. Not even an official date."

"Have you?"

"No. I don't want to scare her away."

"Look at it this way. If you don't tell her, you lose her. If you do tell her and she's not down for it, you still lose her. But if you tell her and she feels the same, you might get everything you want. So, you're really no worse off by speaking up."

He'd made a really great point.

"You are so different from when I first met you."

"Things change, my friend." I felt like he was referring to us both leaving the Teams. "Sometimes, for the better."

"You might be right."

"No *might be* about it, fucker."

I laughed.

"Oh, by the way, Addison's on the phone with Olivia. She stopped and picked you up dinner. That's why she didn't answer her phone."

I growled, "You could have told me that right away, asshole."

"And let you get away with ignoring your feelings? Dream on."

"When I see you again, I'm going to—"

"Thank me. I know. And you're welcome. Gotta go. Bye."

I looked at my phone. Maddox had hung up on me.

He had it all wrong. I wasn't going to thank him. I was going to kick his ass because I knew he was right, smug bastard.

And as I watched Olivia pull into the driveway, I had no idea how I was going to tell her that I loved her.

42

OLIVIA

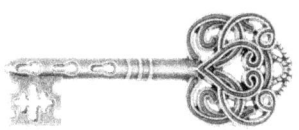

I leaned back in my chair and looked up at my office ceiling.

Something was up with Tommy.

He had acted weird all night. Not quite standoffish. It was almost as if he was afraid of me. But when we had gone to bed and turned out the light, he'd made love to me like he didn't want to let go.

I laughed. I didn't know when my thoughts had changed from *fucking* Tommy to *making love* to him. Probably around the time when he'd made me feel protected but not smothered.

He was doing a number on my heart.

And that scared the crap out of me.

I didn't know what to do about it. I would love it if he moved to Iowa. After all, he'd told me that Virginia didn't hold much for him anymore. But he'd also told me he could never live in Brook Creek. If he wasn't going to move to be close to his good friend, then he probably wasn't going to move.

My cell phone rang at that moment, pulling me from my thoughts.

"Hello?"

It was one of the officers assigned to my case. "We thought you should know that the license plate matched those of Gary Scott. When we went to speak to him and his wife, she broke down and confessed to harassing you."

"Oh. Wow."

"She also confessed to killing her daughter."

I sat up so fast that the back of my chair sprang forward with a loud thump.

"She said she was fighting with Annabelle about her boyfriend. In a fit of rage, she picked up one of the gardener's tools and threw it at Annabelle as she walked away. It hit her in the head. Mrs. Scott claimed it was an accident. She had just wanted to stop her daughter from leaving. We haven't confirmed it yet, but we believe the tool transferred the gardener's DNA onto the daughter. Mrs. Scott's DNA was on her daughter, too, but since they lived together, it was dismissed. Mrs. Scott had fired the gardener later that day, which is why the DNA didn't match any of the employees."

And why it hadn't matched my client's. But the officer and I both already known that.

"Thank you for letting me know." I hung up the phone and sat, stunned.

"Derek," I called over my intercom, "get in here."

He came sprinting in. "What?"

"You'll never guess what I just found out."

When I finished relaying the conversation to Derek, he said, "I never saw that coming."

"You and me both."

The phone on Derek's desk rang. "I'd better get that."

Ten seconds later, he was back. "You'll never guess who's on the phone for you."

"Who?"

"The Scotts' lawyer."

"Put him through."

"I was calling to let you know we're dropping the lawsuit," the Scotts' lawyer said.

No shit. "It should have never been filed in the first place."

"We're just going to have to agree to disagree on that."

"I suppose so. But you might want to warn your clients that we still might be seeing each other again soon."

"How so?"

"In light of the information I received this morning, Tate Garrett has a very strong case for defamation."

He cleared his throat. "Let me talk to my clients and get back to you. We might be able to work something out."

"You do that. I'll be waiting to hear back from you."

I hung up the phone, feeling very good for my client.

Yet a sudden sadness came over me. With Miranda Scott in custody, there was no reason for Tommy to stay with me anymore.

I picked up the phone and dialed Tate to tell him the unbelievable news.

I'd worry about my feelings for Tommy later.

———

When Tommy walked into my office at five thirty on the dot, my stomach was in knots. I had surrounded myself with research on new cases, so I wouldn't have to think about him leaving.

"Hey, Liv," he said, coming over and kissing me.

He seemed on high alert, almost like he was nervous.

Oh no. He didn't know how to tell me he was going back to Brook Creek.

Earlier, I had called Tommy after finishing up with Tate. When I told him the news from the police, he had so much relief in his voice that it almost hurt. I'd thought he had liked spending time with me.

But maybe he was like every other guy I'd dated and couldn't get past how bad I was in bed.

I hadn't thought about that in a long time because I felt more open while having sex with Tommy than anyone else from my past.

But maybe I was doomed to "never truly satisfy a guy," as one ex had told me.

I quickly looked down at my desk, frantically trying to focus on something other than the feeling of wanting to cry.

"Are you ready to get out of here?" he asked me. "There's something I need to talk to you about, especially now that the threats have stopped for good. I thought maybe we could go to dinner somewhere and—"

"I'm sorry. Since the story broke on the news, I've been flooded with new client requests. I can't go to dinner tonight."

Yes, I was lying. My name hadn't come up on the news. But Tommy didn't need to know that.

"I understand you probably need to get back to Brook Creek. You don't have to wait around for me if you want to head back tonight. I can call an Uber or get a ride from someone in the office." My voice started to wobble toward the end, and I knew there was no way I was going to be able to hold back my tears.

I lifted my leg, and my knee rammed against the top of

my desk. "*Ow. Damn it. That hurt.*" I had done it to give me an excuse to cry, except I had actually managed to hurt myself.

The floodgates opened, and there was no holding back my emotions now.

Tommy came around to my side of the desk and swung me around to face him. He got down on his haunches. "Where did you hurt yourself?"

I pointed to my left knee.

He lifted my skirt and kissed it.

It only made me cry harder.

"Hey, I think you'll be okay." He felt all around my lower thigh and knee. "It looks like it's just going to be a bruise."

"I'll take some painkillers. I'll be fine." If only the painkillers could reach my heart. I pushed against his shoulders. "But I really should get back to work." Maybe if I buried myself deeply enough in cases, it wouldn't hurt so much.

Tommy stood and rounded my desk once more, so we were on opposite sides. He stood there with his hands on his hips for a minute and then nodded. "We'll talk later then."

No, I wanted to scream. *We don't need to talk. You don't have to explain anything to me. You can just leave. I don't need excuses.*

But he was already out the door.

I took several deep breaths, grabbed a tissue to wipe my face and blow my nose, and went back to work.

It took me about fifteen minutes to put all my concentration into my work, but I did it. The endorphin release from crying had actually helped because I was feeling a lot calmer now and like the world wouldn't end with Tommy leaving.

I would get through it, and life would go on.

I picked up a slip of paper with a client's name, and underneath, it said, *Possible civil rights case.*

Interesting.

I wasn't a civil rights lawyer, but a couple of our associates were. I could always be second chair if the case warranted it.

I turned to my computer and pulled up Google. It was always the first place I did research because there was usually a plethora of information out there.

I was about ten articles deep into the possible case when I felt someone enter my office.

I didn't turn to look because I was too busy reading.

"Do you want me to go back to Brook Creek?"

Somewhere in the back of my mind, I realized it was Tommy. But I didn't have time to talk right now.

So, I did what I always did when I was busy. I answered questions as fast as I could, so I could get whoever was talking to leave me alone. "No, I don't."

I went back to reading, clicking on a Reddit thread. Those were always fascinating because they could have wild theories and were out there, but sometimes, the people were pretty close to the truth with their guesses.

"Do you want to see me go back to Virginia?"

"No," I answered, irritation making my tone clipped.

"Good, because I don't want to go back. You know why?"

I sighed. "No."

"Because I love you, and I think you love me, too. Do you love me, Olivia?"

I gritted my teeth. *Can't he tell I'm in the middle of something important?*

"Yes, I love you. Now, will you please go away?"

Part of me heard Tommy laugh, but our conversation didn't really hit me until he walked over and pushed my laptop cover closed.

"Hey," I said, looking up at him.

He was grinning. Something had just happened.

"Oh crap. What did I miss?"

"You told me once that when you're busy at work, you answer things quite honestly. So, you, my dear, just gave me some great information."

I ran back the conversation in my mind and gasped. I cupped my hands over my mouth.

And damn it, I started crying again.

"Did…did you say you…" I couldn't quite finish.

Tommy took my hand and pulled me up out of my seat. He guided me around my desk and into his arms. "I said I love you. I don't want to go back to Virginia. I don't even want to go back to Brook Creek. I want to stay here with you. And you might have let it slip that you love me, too."

"But what about the bedroom stuff?"

His brow furrowed in confusion. "What bedroom stuff?"

I started playing with his T-shirt. "Me. I'm not so good in there. I've had numerous exes break up with me because of that."

The guy had the nerve to throw his head back and laugh.

"Ouch," I couldn't help but say.

He quickly shook his head back and forth, but he couldn't quite stop his laughter. "No, Liv, I'm not laughing at *you*. I'm laughing at *them*."

"You are?"

"Yes, because you're the best goddamn lay I've ever had."

I frowned. "Do you have to be so crass?"

He laughed again. "You like it when I'm crass."

I smiled. "Maybe I do."

He snorted. "No maybe about it."

I took a deep breath. "What about work? You don't have a job."

"I was thinking maybe you'd like to hire me?"

"For what? I already told you, the firm is not going to pay for a bodyguard. And I don't really need one anymore."

"I thought I could fill that investigator position. I looked into it. I need to get certified, but I don't need a degree or anything. But if you'd put up with me for a while, I think I'd like to work on getting my criminal justice degree if I'm going to do this full-time."

I leaned back in his arms and studied him. "You're not just settling for this job because you want to be close to me, are you?"

"No. The other day, when I was knocking on doors and calling the bank, I loved it. I haven't had that much fun working in a long time. Is it as fun as being a SEAL? No. But nothing will be. And this is the closest I've ever gotten. I think I'd like to explore it."

"I think that sounds like an amazing idea." I wrapped my arms around his neck and kissed him.

Tommy pushed me up against my desk. "I think it's time for some celebration sex."

EPILOGUE

TOMMY

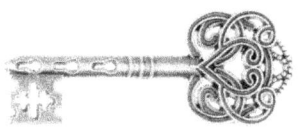

SEVERAL YEARS LATER

*M*addox and I bumped fists. "Ready to beat the Donaldsons once again?" I asked.

He laughed. "Will they ever learn that they're not going to win?"

I looked over at Frank and his cousins with their heads down as they strategized. "I don't think so."

At this point, it was becoming an annual tradition to beat them every year at Brook Days.

We separated, and I got into my position on the field. I glanced over at the sidelines, where Olivia was rubbing her belly as she spoke to Addison. Addison was patting the back of her new daughter while Spencer and Thane ran literal circles around the two ladies.

My Olivia was due in a month and a half, and I couldn't wait. At first, she hadn't been certain that she wanted kids. I didn't push because I knew how important her career was to her. But after I got my associate's degree in criminal justice and passed my certification with the National Association of Legal Investigators, I thought she'd decided it would be a good time to try.

We'd gotten pregnant the first month, and knowing that a part of me was growing in my wife's womb was better than any mission I'd ever gone on in the military.

Olivia looked over at me and smiled.

Every single day, I understood Maddox's words more and more.

"Things change. Sometimes, for the better."

He'd sure gotten that right.

TAKE ME IN THE NIGHT EXCERPT
MADDOX

I didn't know who was more surprised—Addison or me.

I certainly hadn't expected her to walk through the door. When Foster had told me that he was going to get a lawyer, I had been so surprised that Brook Creek had one that I didn't even think to ask who the person was.

She turned around. "Please close the door," she said to Whitlock, her voice firm and full of authority.

It wasn't the only firm thing in the room.

Whitlock shot me a dirty look before closing the door, and Addison turned back around.

She gestured toward the table. "Can we please sit?"

I shrugged, pulled out the chair closest to me, and sat.

Addison did the same and took out a notebook and pen from her purse. She started writing things down, and I took the opportunity to study her. Her chestnut hair had been down to her ass in high school, but now, it was only a couple of inches past her shoulders. Her breasts strained against the top, and I was pretty sure they'd gotten bigger since I last saw her, which was saying something because she'd had a pretty impressive set of tits back then.

And I couldn't see it now, but I had noticed her nice, round ass before she sat down. Her black pants were so tight that I was ninety-nine percent positive she was going commando or wearing a thong. No panty lines for Addison.

She looked up at me. "So, can you tell me what's going on?"

"Foster picked me up from the airport. I was driving my brother's car when I got pulled over. Next thing I knew, Whitlock was putting handcuffs on me."

"What for?"

I scowled. "Fuck if I know. That asshole's always had a hard-on for me."

She sighed. "What was his reason? What did he tell you?"

I snorted. "That I was speeding."

"Were you?"

"I was going fifty-eight in a fifty-five."

"Anything else unusual?"

"Other than the fact that I was driving? No."

"As I recall, you didn't always follow traffic laws."

Her comment had me thinking of all the times we'd driven around in my beat-up Chevy truck and the things we'd done in it besides driving. It seemed Addison was thinking the same thing.

I totally recognized the look on her face.

It was the same one she used to give me before she pulled down my pants and sucked my cock into her mouth.

I'd grown up around adults with loose morals, so it was no shock that I'd lost my virginity at fourteen to my mom's friend's daughter. She was sixteen when she came to my house, looking for her mother. Her mom and my mom had left twenty-four hours earlier to go on a bender.

So, Sheila took me to the room I shared with my brother and showed me the things she liked to do in bed. I lasted all of twenty seconds before blowing my load, but thankfully, Sheila gave me a few more rounds that I used to make it up to her.

That was just the beginning. For a while, I had fucked anything that I could.

But Addison had grown up completely different from me. She had been a virgin when she and I started dating. Every-thing she knew in the bedroom, she'd learned from me. Including how to give the best fucking blow jobs.

I tilted my head to the side. I wondered if she still gave good head.

My eighteen-year-old self demanded I find out. My thirty-year-old self didn't need the complications of being inside Addison Graham again.

"Yeah, well, I've changed along with my driving habits. I was going the speed limit. He had no reason to pull me over."

She wrote the information down and stood. I stared at her ass as she pounded on the door.

"Sheriff, come in here, please."

The door opened thirty seconds later.

"What do you need, Counselor?"

"My client said he was doing fifty-eight in a fifty-five. Give him his speeding ticket, so he can leave."

"Whoa, whoa, whoa. I don't know if he's been drinking."

"Did you give him a Breathalyzer? A sobriety test? Did he smell like alcohol?"

Whitlock gritted his teeth. "No."

"Is he under arrest?"

Whitlock looked pissed. "No."

I shoved my chair back and stood as Addison said, "Then, he's free to leave."

Whitlock stepped around Addison and marched up to my face. "I am going to break you. You're not going to get away with anything like you did twelve years ago."

He was so close; I could smell the stale coffee on his breath despite our six-inch height difference.

I just crossed my arms over my chest and tried not to look bored. This man had no idea the things I'd gone through to be a SEAL. There was nothing he could do to hurt me. I'd already lost everything once, and that was the biggest blow I'd ever taken.

"I didn't get away with anything," I told him.

Movement out of the corner of my vision caught my eye, and I looked over at Addison. She clearly looked confused.

I looked back at Whitlock, who was staring at me, steam practically coming out of his ears. I smacked the top of his arm like we were old friends because I knew it would piss him off, and I walked around him. "Later, Whitlock. Call me when you're ready to break me. You know where to find me."

I walked past Addison and nodded my thanks. I found Foster waiting for me outside the sheriff's office, pacing with panic all over his face.

His look turned to relief when he saw me. "Oh, thank God."

"You can thank Addison."

I heard the sound of her heels coming up behind me.

"I didn't really do anything," she said as she came to stand beside me. "He was just trying to intimidate Maddox, I think."

Foster burst out laughing. "What a putz. My brother is a Navy SEAL and has been to countries like Afghanistan and Iraq. He is not scared of Sheriff Whitlock."

Addison whipped her head and looked at me. "You're a SEAL?"

"Yep." There was no point in denying it.

She turned her whole body toward me. "What did Whitlock mean by, 'You're not going to get away with anything like you did twelve years ago'? Have you been in the Navy this whole time? Did you even go to prison?"

I just raised an eyebrow at her. She didn't need me to confirm the answer she already knew.

She looked at Foster. "How long have you known this?"

ABOUT THE AUTHOR

R.L. Kenderson is two best friends writing under one name.

Renae has always loved reading, and in third grade, she wrote her first poem where she learned she might have a knack for this writing thing. Lara remembers sneaking her grandmother's Harlequin novels when she was probably too young to be reading them, and since then, she knew she wanted to write her own.

When they met in college, they bonded over their love of reading and the TV show *Charmed*. What really spiced up their friendship was when Lara introduced Renae to romance novels. When they discovered their first vampire romance, they knew there would always be a special place in their hearts for paranormal romance. After being unable to find certain storylines and characteristics they wanted to read about in the hundreds of books they consumed, they decided to write their own.

One lives in the Minneapolis-St. Paul area and the other in the Kansas City area where they both work in the medical field during the day and a sexy author by night. They communicate through phone, email, and whole lot of messaging.

You can find them at http://www.rlkenderson.com, Facebook, Instagram, TikTok, and Goodreads. Join their reader group! Or you can email them at rlkenderson@rlkenderson

.com, or sign up for their newsletter. They always love hearing from their readers.

www.ingramcontent.com/pod-product-compliance
Lightning Source LLC
Chambersburg PA
CBHW060422180626
46817CB00007B/2627